Heart of Community

Book #2

Neighbor to Neighbor Series

Sue Batton Leonard

Published 2021.

Printed in the United States of America.

ISBN 978-1-950647-86-6

Publisher's Cataloging-in-Publication data

Names: Leonard, Sue Batton, author.
Title: Heart of community / Sue Batton Leonard.
Series: Neighbor to Neighbor
Description: Parker, CO: Book Crafters, 2021.
Identifiers: ISBN: 978-1-950647-86-6
Subjects: LCSH Friendship--Fiction. | Women--Fiction. | Christian fiction. | BISAC FICTION / Christian / Contemporary
Classification: LCC PS3612 .E66 H43 2021 | DDC 813.6--dc23

Publishing assistance by BookCrafters, Parker, Colorado.
www.bookcrafters.net

I dedicate this book to all hometown heroes and essential workers in communities across America who share their spirit and talents for the benefit of others to make this world a better place.

Author Disclaimer Statement

Heart of Community – Neighbor to Neighbor Series Book #2 is a work of fiction.

"Belle Aire" is a composite of numerous historic Main Street America communities the author has visited and admired throughout her travels. All characters, businesses, and events which are part of the narrative are fictional and a product of the author's imagination. Any likeness to real people, places, events or businesses which are part of the storyline are purely coincidental.

Won't you be a good neighbor and tell others about this heart-warming story?

And in the Beginning....

Chapter 1 from *Sew the Heart*

Book 1
Neighbor to Neighbor Series

"I'VE HAD IT," MOXIE SAID OUT LOUD TO HERSELF, wiping the tears from her eyes with the arm of her black long sleeve tee-shirt. Pitch black mascara ran from her eyes all over her cheeks. She had no idea how long she had been walking along the leaf-covered railroad tracks. Stopping several times that morning, she sat between the rails, inert, unable to move ahead, lost in thought.

Every day for the past few months, she walked a portion of the railroad tracks from where she lived far outside the southern Colorado town of Kellenville to her part-time job at a donut shop in Hopewell. As the crow flies she lived closer to Hopewell.

With each step one more bad memory was stirred up. Although each mile along the railroad tracks held exquisite views of the Sangre de Cristo Mountains, with fourteen thousand foot peaks, she couldn't find any beauty in her surroundings. She was too despondent. It was as if the girl was walking between rows of tall cornstalks on flat fields, without the ability to see out. With each step it was as if she went deeper into a dark tunnel. Memories replayed of relationships gone wrong, the teasing she had endured all her life, the insecure feelings she'd had when she realized her life was so different and empty compared to some of her school mates. Although lots of friends came from broken households, she wondered why none of her friends were screwed up like her. And then there was her buddy Alexis who was bounced around to different foster homes just as much, but Alexis didn't seem to have any trouble handling it. She aced everything and went off to college on scholarship money.

Moxie recalled each time she was moved from foster home to foster home. Once, after four years when she was settled into a loving environment that looked like it might become permanent, it had come to naught. Again she was uprooted when "the household circumstances changed" and her foster parents decided not to adopt her. There were so many changes in "household circumstances" throughout her lifetime, she wasn't even sure how old she was when she was moved from the southeastern part of the country to the Sangre de Christo Mountains in Colorado.

All she knew for sure was she hated her life and wanted to end it. If the train barreled down the track, she'd let it sweep her under. All the pain would be gone and she wouldn't have to deal with having to support herself. Now an adult, she was really on her own and every false sense of belonging to a family was gone. She never felt more alone in her life.

I don't even know how to support myself, Moxie thought as she kicked the leaves covering the tracks with her worn shoes with soles which had begun to separate between the layers. She felt like she had been on her own trying to fend for herself ever since she was a small child. She'd gotten so little support from anyone who was supposed to be her guardian. Even her "friends" had abandoned her as she'd moved from place to place. Only thing she had to be thankful for was meeting the old lady with the donuts, Miss Eunice, who was nice enough to let her live in her one room studio apartment in her guest house. For the time being, anyway. Even if the place was out in the boonies and not near public transportation, at least she wasn't living on the streets anymore.

Moxie squatted down in the dried aspen leaves

and circled her arms around her head, grabbing both elbows with her hands as if she was trying form a protective orb or cocoon around herself. She inhaled the earthy odors of the fall season and thought how she'd like to dig a hole and bury herself. She lost her balance and just as she was about to keel over from her squatting position, she caught herself with her right hand as she placed it on the ground in the pile of crunchy leaves. She swept the leaves aside and when she did, she saw something gleaming. Although it was dawn and the sun was a few minutes from rising, the contrast between her black fingernail polish and the shiny object caught her attention. At first she thought the shiny object was part of the rail, but she realized it moved when she touched it. What was a silver-colored charm bracelet doing between the railroad ties?

Moxie picked up the bracelet, and as she did a small silver cross fell off. She knew where she was headed—to the pawn place as soon as her shift ended at the donut shop.

She stood and hurried along, not taking time to really look at the jewelry. She stuffed the bracelet and the unattached charm into the pocket of her drab olive corduroy jacket that was so old, there wasn't any nap left to it. She stepped up her pace so she wouldn't be late because she couldn't risk being fired. All she had was the little money she made at the donut shop. How Moxie hated putting on the foolish pink and white uniform which made her feel ridiculous like a Miss Goody Two Shoes. She couldn't expect any hot-to-trot man to look at her twice dressed like that.

And so the Story Continues....

Heart of Community

Book 2
Neighbor to Neighbor Series

Sue Batton Leonard

Chapter 1

MOXIE CLIMBED INTO BED feeling weary and content. She reached over and took her journal out of her bedside table and wrote: It felt glorious tonight at the Neighbor-to-Neighbor meeting to be in a new community and finally reach the point when you walk in the doors you know all the kindhearted people. My heart pumped the warmth I was feeling throughout my body. My head felt like a lit lightbulb radiating heat and my toes felt as if they wore a pair of fuzzy cashmere socks. Matt and I heard so many words of encouragement about the work we are doing as we lent a hand setting up for dinner in Fellowship Hall and putting out chairs at the far end of the room for the business meeting.

Moxie closed her journal and put it on top of the bedside table. She sank into the pile of soft eiderdown pillows leaning against the upholstered headboard, closed her eyes, and breathed in deeply. How far she'd come in one year's time. She lay there remembering vividly her conversation with her friend Matt just over a year ago. It was the day she walked out of Attorney Loyal Roberts' office to Matt's car where he was waiting for her after two wills were read.

"Bane or Blessing?" Matt asked as Moxie threw herself onto the passenger seat like a twenty-five-pound sack of flour.

"I don't know. I don't know," cried out Moxie cupping her shaking hands and covering her eyes.

"Whoa, whoa, whoa! I guess I asked the wrong question."

"Matt, just take me home, will ya?"

Matt started the car and drove silently, headed in the direction of Moxie's apartment over her sewing shop.

"There you go." Matt stopped the car and quickly opened the driver's side door and hustled around to open the passenger door for Moxie.

"Oh, Matt, I'm sorry. I'm just so overwhelmed. I don't know what to think of anything. I mean... just when I thought...now, this happens."

Matt looked at Moxie's confused expression on her face. He no longer thought of himself as her boss, but as a person whose friendship was growing dearer.

"Please come in, will you? I'm not sure I want to be alone right now."

"Ok, Moxie, gladly." They climbed the stairs slowly. Moxie felt heaviness in her legs and slightly dizzy. She unlocked the door, and they went in and sat side by side on the sofa.

Suddenly, Moxie burst out laughing. "Wacky ladies!"

"What? What is it Moxie?" Every time Moxie began to explain she broke up into laughter again.

"Must be pretty funny. Share it. Please! Tell me." It felt good to hear her laughter.

Moxie finally took control of her outbursts. "Oh, it's just something Eunice said to me one time. When you asked me how my meeting was – bane or blessing, I just remembered the conversation."

"Oh. Go on."

"One day, Eunice and I were discussing aging and how she and her dear lady friend Mildred were getting up in their years. Eunice looked at me in all seriousness and said, "Moxie, I do believe no matter what, we will meet again when you join Mildred and me in heaven. And by the way," she said, "I'll be sitting on the right-hand side of God, the Father, and the chocolate fountain. That's where all blessings flow."

Matt burst out laughing and Moxie lost her composure again.

"Well, if that isn't a Eunice-ism!" Matt was well familiar with the old lady Eunice. What a stitch. She was a steady daily customer at the donut shop where he and Moxie worked years ago. She came in at the end of every day for stale chocolate donuts for "her Toby." Whoever Toby was.

After the laughter subsided Moxie turned to Matt. "How about something to eat? I've got a whole refrigerator full of funeral food I need to get rid of. It just keeps coming."

"Are you gonna eat?"

"No, not right now. My stomach is too churned up." Moxie's gaze went to the window which looked all fogged up. Matt watched the corners of her mouth turn downward again into sadness.

"Don't get up! I can help myself." Matt had become quite comfortable at Moxie's. Over the past several weeks, he'd become Moxie's rock as he mourned with her over the loss of her two dear lady friends, Mildred and Eunice." As soon as he read the headlines in the *Hopewell Weekly* announcing "Two Local Women Killed Taking a Chocolate Joy Ride," he got in his car and went right over to Moxie's apartment.

Moxie was so grateful for his presence. Without him she may have sunken into a dark abyss never to climb out again.

Matt opened the refrigerator and looked in.

"Holy Cow, Moxie. Look at the pasta salad. Good grief! The bowl it's in is as big as a claw-footed bathtub."

"I told you I had funeral food up the ying-yang, didn't I?" There was no funeral for Eunice and Mildred with a requisite funeral luncheon following. The two women had left separate letters instructing Attorney Loyal Thomas nearly the same. "When my time comes to an end, no big hullabaloo." No one, they both said, could match the fun the two old women had created for themselves during their years of friendship. "So, don't even try to have a memorial celebration without me," said Eunice in her letter. Quite frankly, Moxie was relieved. They had both outlived almost all their peers.

"You know the people of Hopewell, Matt. They're well practiced whether or not there's a viewing and funeral. As soon as they see obits in the paper, they go into action. Ovens are fired up, pots begin to boil, and casserole dishes are greased up. The food...there has been no let up. And with two obits with a sensational headline of two community favorites all in one day, double every recipe."

"Yeah, and you know as well as me, tongues are still wagging over the headline and tears are still dripping." Moxie nodded in agreement.

“Salivatory glands are still drooling for funeral food. That I know for sure. An entourage of people are still coming in the door daily at Sew the Heart to pay their respects and share a repast. My staff and I have become vessels for a whole lot of deeply shared emotion. Oh, how everyone in the area loved those two women!”

“Did you ever know they knew so many people?”

“They sure knew how to make connections. Mildred often lamented how people aren’t neighborly any more like they used to be when she was a kid. But the number of people who have stopped to pay their respects has been astounding. Each one promising “they’d rather honor the two women in some way other than sitting through an ungodly funeral or memorial service.”

“Not quite sure what to make of that.”

“No, me neither.”

“Help yourself, Matt. There’s ham, turkey salad, wings, green salad, and casseroles just waiting to be nuked. I don’t know what all. Just nose around. And desserts! I told the girls downstairs, we are going to have to do a community cookie, pie and cake walk just to get rid of the sweets. Afterall, Miss Eunice is not here to consume all the chocolate cakes, chocolate pies and chocolate chip cookies.”

Matt loaded up a full plate and settled back

down beside Moxie. "Thanks. I guess I came to the right place. I am hungry." Moxie sat quietly until Matt could get some food in his belly.

"So, how ya doin'? Are you sleeping any better?" asked Matt. By the dark circles under Moxies eyes, he already knew the answer.

"Some nights I am when the shoulda, coulda, woulda's don't creep back in."

"Did the autopsies come back?"

"Yeah... they did." Moxie said, sadly looking down at her lap.

"Feel like talking about it?"

Frankly, Moxie was glad he asked. "Well, the autopsies didn't detect any medical reasons why Eunice's pink Cadillac slammed head-on into a tree and nothing mechanically wrong with the vehicle either."

"Nothing? And no evidence of alcohol or drugs in either bodies?"

"Nope."

"Did the police mention any suspicions or motives?"

"Only thing they found was a large stash of opened chocolates in the back seat. In search of answers, the box of chocolates was sent to the lab, and every ingredient checked out fine. The chocolates were as labeled, 90% cacao.

"There is where my woulda, coulda, shoulda's

kick in." Moxie turned her head away from Matt and wiped tears.

"What do you mean?"

"I feel like it's all my fault. Several days prior to the accident I'd given Eunice the huge box of gourmet chocolates...ha, what a friend I am. I completely spaced out and forgot about her addiction. She's had a life-long problem with sweets, especially chocolate."

"I had no idea! But Moxie, what about all those chocolate donuts she came in to buy daily but took home for her Toby to eat?"

Moxie didn't say anything. She just looked at Matt.

"Ahhh... oh, oh, now I see. I'm a little slow. They probably weren't really for 'her Toby,' were they?'"

Moxie, shook her head no.

"Matt, don't you see how I might feel responsible?"

"How so, Moxie? Tell me."

"I was only trying to do something special for Miss Eunice. She'd been a wonderful landlord and lifesaver who picked me up from the depths of despair and rescued me by giving me a place to live and a bright future."

"Very kind woman she was, from what I knew of her," said Matt.

"When I saw the beautifully embellished box top with ribbons and flowers containing fancy dark gourmet chocolates, I knew I wanted to treat Eunice to a large box, the likes of which she'd never had before. I've never known her to eat anything other than low-grade chocolates you'd give out to children on Halloween – a bag of foil wrapped candy costing $2.99 for sixty pieces."

"Or greasy chocolate donuts I cooked," Matt added.

"Once Eunice got a taste of the exquisite candy, she said, 'Oh my dear, Moxie, I'm swearing off anything less than 90% cacao. From here on out, I'm only going to ingest chocolate that increases my iron, magnesium and zinc levels and has high antioxidant qualities.'"

Matt howled with laughter.

"That day I gave Miss Eunice the present changed everything for all three of us – Miss Eunice, Miss Mildred and me. A few bites into the chocolates and Eunice and Mildred looked at each other and said, "What are we waiting for?" They decided that very day it was time to return to something they had done in their younger years – take joy rides.

"This time, we will have real purpose," Miss Eunice said with a huge mischievous smile on her face. "Let's spend the rest of our lives visiting chocolate shops across the country in search of the best of the best!"

"Let's start tomorrow. And, while we're on the road, we may as well be in search of extraordinary fabrics which will make prize winning quilts. Maybe some batiks." said Miss Mildred. "And tea rooms, we will hit them all."

"Oh yes, yes!" the two women said in unison.

"Yes Ma'am!" said Miss Eunice, taking a sniff inward. "I can smell those confectionery shops now! Oh, we will have a fabulous time." I shook my head and stifled a laugh when Miss Eunice began drooling, but I had no idea how the two women's plan would change our lives.

"I was all onboard with their idea, we three had recently had a conversation about the sewing shop and our three-way partnership. We had made some crucial decisions."

"Like what?" Matt's piercing blue eyes looked at Moxie in consternation.

"We decided the shop was in dire need of a facelift. This meant again weeding out fabrics which had been sitting in the shop for some time. We needed to carry newer designs being very, very selective in replacing the old with an eye for what would make outstanding art quilt designs which are becoming ever more popular. The next generation of quilters want fresh fabrics in the marketplace. Not the same ole, same ole."

"Can I interject and ask a question? How long had they owned the business?"

"Oh, forever and a day, Matt, but I'm not sure exactly. All I know is some of the inventory was ancient."

Miss Eunice said to me before they left in the car that fatal morning, "We will be as discriminating with our fabric choices as our chocolates."

I tried to get them to be not so rash and to give me a few more days to discuss what I needed to do while they were away, but they wouldn't listen. "It's settled!" said Miss Mildred. "After all, our CFA has said 'we may as well go enjoy our final years by mixing business with pleasure.' It's what we've worked so hard for. And we know the future of the shop is in good hands with you Moxie." They waved their hands, "Tootle loo," they said, and off they went.

I stood there with my mouth wide open wondering what a CFA stood for.

Matt looked at Moxie and didn't answer, he knew who their CFA was. His office was upstairs across the hall from Matt's in the real estate building.

"Knowing those two women, CFA probably meant their "Chocolate & Fabric Advisor."

Matt chuckled. Moxie's naivete sometimes surprised him and always charmed him.

"So, Moxie, you still haven't told me how any of this is your fault. Who was at the wheel?"

"Eunice."

"So, from what you told me, only conclusion I can draw is that Eunice, the driver, was on a sugar high and the two were horsing around – being, well... just Eunice and Mildred." Matt grabbed both of Moxies hands and looked her directly in the eye. "I think you can rely on what you've been told as the God's honest truth. No more wouldas, shouldas or couldas. Please don't take blame for what was strictly an unfortunate accident of two adults who made their own decisions. God determines when our time on this earth is up."

"Oh Matt, thank you for your note of grace. That's exactly what the police officers and investigators said. They said to always remember, Eunice and Mildred left this world when they were on the ultimate joy ride of their life."

Chapter 2

FROM 3 A.M. ONWARD Moxie had been awake checking the time hourly. Finally, at 7 a.m. she decided to call Matt figuring he'd be rising anyway to start his day.

"Matt, here."

"Hi Matt, its Moxie."

"Well, good morning, lovely lady." *Hmmm.* Moxie thought, *no one has ever called ME that before.*

"I had that dreaded conversation with Beverly, my sewing shop manager, yesterday."

"Oh yeah, really?"

Moxie looked again at the clock. "Oh, Matt, I'm so sorry. Nothing like hitting you up with a long discussion the second you've opened your eyes."

"Moxie. This apologizing has got to stop. You act as if you aren't worthy of my attention. Like I told you last week, I am here for you anytime.

Hey, meet for coffee this morning? Would ya like that?"

"Sure!"

"Shall I come to Hopewell, or do you want to come here?"

"I'll gladly come to you, Matt. Every chance I get to visit my new community is a chance to meet people in Belle Aire."

"What? What did you just say Moxie?"

"You heard me!" Moxie said with more gusto than she expected.

"Say it again Moxie. Plant it in your brain and root it deeply. Go ahead...I am waiting."

"Oh, all right. Damn, you can be bossy." Moxie did as Matt requested. She repeated her statement about her new community.

"Morning Glory's at 9 o'clock?"

"Perfect! See you then."

Moxie showered and dressed putting on her sleeveless pale apricot dropped-waist dress made of crinkly rayon crepe for the hot day ahead. At the last minute she decided to accessorize with a vintage piece of jewelry Miss Mildred had given her years back. It was a beautiful reminder of who she lost and Mildred's friendship. That was what she most treasured.

An hour and a half later, Matt met Moxie at the door of Morning Glory's with a hug.

“Don’t you look nice this morning, Moxie. That’s an interesting piece of jewelry.”

“Thanks, Matt. Mildred gave me this pendant watch. It looks kinda nice with this bo-ho dress, don’t you think?”

“I do. You look well put together today.” Moxie smiled as they found their way to the seats the waitress led them to.

After the waitress took their orders, Matt was as direct as Moxie had been earlier jumping right into the discussion of Moxie's moving. There was no beating around the proverbial bush.

“Have I got this right? You are ready to join me in here in Belle Aire?”

“Yes and yes. Last night I made a decisive decision.”

“Just like that? No going back and second guessing yourself?”

“Nope. Why would I do that?”

Matt shrugged his shoulders.

“It’s not the direction I am going. Onward Christian soldiers as Eunice used to say. Besides, what more have I got to lose? Do you realize the opportunity I’ve been given? It’s time for me to find my own tribe of contemporaries, not meaning any disrespect to Eunice and Mildred. I see Belle Aire as the perfect place to establish a new life. From the letters Eunice and Mildred left behind they blessed me with guilt-free reign to do as I please with the business."

"And? What will that be? If you don't mind me asking?"

"It's practically settled. My shop manager finally has all her ducks in a row. She is buying me out. Free and clear. Beverly couldn't be a better person."

Matt stood from his seat, came around the table and gave Moxie a high five and a warm hug.

"Well, it is a glorious morning, isn't it Moxie?"

"Yes, it is! Except for the bad pun." As they ate, Moxie and Matt talked about what it would be like to live in the same community.

When the waitress appeared at the tableside to give them the bill, Matt said, "Nora, will you bring one of your signature Morning Glory muffins to go for our new resident of this community?"

"Sure. Hi, I'm Nora, pleased to meet you." She stuck out her hand. Moxie raised hers to meet it.

"I'm Moxie."

"Welcome, new neighbor. I'll be right back with your muffin and I'll leave it at the register in a white pastry bag."

"Now Mr. Realtor, I need you to find me a place to plant myself."

"I'm on it. Ready to go? I see your muffin waiting for us at the register. I've got to get to work."

They scrambled over to the register by the door, Matt insisted on paying the bill. They said their goodbyes in the parking lot and went their separate ways to their cars. Before heading back to Hopewell to continue packing, Moxie took a quick joy ride through town. Settlement day was two months away and she'd be handing the keys to the sewing shop over to Beverly and opening the door to a new life. There was so much to do.

Chapter 3

"REALLY GLAD WE CAN HAVE this discussion today, Moxie, so I will have a better idea of what you are looking for here in town. I want to find a place that absolutely suits you and the goals you have for yourself."

For the next several hours Matt and Moxie batted around ideas and looked over listings. "Moxie, it may take some time. You do know about the rezoning, right?"

"No, Matt, I don't. Tell me."

"Well, there's going to be a redistricting of properties that lie just outside of the commercial zone. They will become mixed use. In other words, more properties could be used either as residential or business. So that could open up a lot more you may be interested in."

"But how long will that take?"

"Not sure. But the way I see it we shouldn't rush."

"Shouldn't rush? Matt, I have to be out of my place within six weeks."

"Yes, I know. We could always find you temporary living arrangements."

"Oh, Matt. I only want to move once!" Moxie could feel her blood pressure rising and her shrill voice indicated she was more stressed than she realized.

"Moxie, let's go over what we've been discussing. #1 top priority is you want to be within walking distance of Main Street, and #2 a mixed-use property might be desirable."

"Yep."

"Well then, again, by waiting for the rezoning it will open up more possibilities. Moxie, do you understand how highly desired this historic area is?"

"The moment I stepped foot in this town I could feel it was something special and there's no question I want to be here."

"Then, be willing to wait so you don't settle on something just to get in. Make sure the shoe fits."

Listen to Him. Moxie said to herself.

"Sometimes providence comes knocking on our door. I'll work hard and you just focus on getting yourself packed up."

"Providence...yeah. That was Miss Mildred's favorite word."

"Was it?"

"Yep. One time Mildred used it one too many times in a day and threw Eunice off the deep end."

"What happened?"

After Mildred had said it for the umpteenth time, Eunice said to her, "Come on Miss Fancy Pants, just say it like it is rather than using your haughty language. It means getting damn lucky!"

"No Eunice," Mildred said, "if you think that's what providence means then you've never experienced it."

"I have too!" said Eunice indignantly. "It's like the time I was walking down the street and suddenly a handful of chocolate kisses landed at my feet, and I had no idea where they came from. I know what your big words mean, and don't tell me I don't!"

Mildred didn't say a word.

"Remember, Mildred, I had a bunch of hard knocks just like you and what saved me, saved you too!"

Matt and Moxie chuckled together. "God, it must have been something spending as much time as you did with them."

"Yeah. It was. But you knew their bantering with one another was all in good fun. They were thick as thieves." *Well, we won't go there,* Moxie thought. Thievin' with her step-brother at the pawn shop was her very least proud moment in life. It was only by God's grace Moxie didn't end up in the slammer with him. Moxie was so glad her years of living with a string of "uneven mothers" as Miss Mildred used to say about her interesting assortment of foster mothers, were over.

Moxie gathered her coat and purse and got ready to leave Matt's real estate office. "Don't lose hope Moxie. It will happen. The right place will come through for me and you."

Chapter 4

MOXIE CLIMBED INTO BED and quietly lay there recalling her day. When the call came in early that morning, she didn't expect to hear from Matt so soon. At least not until he had a property to show her in Belle Aire.

"Moxie, I have a favor to ask of you today. Our monthly Neighbor-to-Neighbor Network meeting, aka NNN, is tonight. The family who normally cooks for us have all fallen sick with the flu. Any interest in donating all that perfectly good funeral food you have in the freezer for the meeting tonight?"

"Oh, God, Matt. That's like music to my ears. Last night I petitioned for a solution of how to unload it without dumping the food in the trash. So many good souls and good cooks worked so hard in their kitchens to make sure I had enough. This is a prayer answered. Believe me."

“Great! everyone will appreciate it. Get the food out of the freezer now.”

“You will join us this evening, won’t you? Otherwise, I’ll come pick the food up. On second thought, do you need me to come help you load it in your car?”

“Not necessary. I'll get the gals at the sewing shop to help me. I keep taking food down to them and they are all complaining the waists on their pants are getting too tight and they are going to have to make new clothing. They'll be as glad as I will to see it all go.”

“Fellowship Hall in the Community Church at 6 p.m. Do you know where the church is?”

“Yes, but I think I’d better come at 5:30 to set it up. And whatever needs to be heated, I’ll bring it already hot.”

“Good thinking.”

What a fun evening it was. But trying to remember people’s names was going to be a challenge. Moxie wasn't used to being around so many people. When she mentioned the friendliness of the crowd to Matt, he said it was “divinely ordained.”

One person gave Moxie a lead on a moving company who he said, “will not rob a woman blind.” Others shared names of good car mechanics, the names of their favorite farm stands for local produce, names of good dentists, and more useful knowledge for a newcomer.

Hands were aplenty to help Moxie carry the food into the church and set it up. They were a jovial bunch immediately taking her into the fold. Even at the business meeting after dinner, never did she feel "you are not one of us." She felt free to offer her two cents worth as someone who hadn't even moved into the community yet.

At the start of the business meeting a woman with wild gray hair came and introduced herself as Johanna Harrison. From all first appearances, she was what Mildred would have called a "questor."

"What is a questor?" Moxie once asked Mildred.

She replied, "Questor is a person trying to find themselves or their next act."

But truthfully, the way Moxie saw it, to Mildred any middle-aged woman who wasn't beautifully coiffed at the hair salon weekly and outfitted in a proper dress, heels and jewelry was considered a "questor."

Mildred called Eunice "an ancient questor." Eunice, who always dressed in thread-bare, out-of-style pant suits that had long ago seen their better days, took great exception to being called an ancient questor.

"Mildred, stop criticizing my appearance. I made each one of these beautiful outfits myself.

You keep saying "they hang and droop." Well, it's no wonder! You won't allow me to have chocolate. I'm practically starving. Did you know if you eat chocolate five times a week, you are fifty-seven percent less likely to have a heart attack?"

"Where did you read that, Eunice?"

"From a very reliable source."

"Yeah, well, tell me the name of it."

"In my favorite rag sheet!"

"Oh, for Pete's sake, Eunice. I hope you don't believe everything you read."

"I'm not an ancient questor, I tell you. I found myself a long time ago, thank you very much, and now I'm just nurturing my nature."

Questor or not, Moxie found her conversation with Johanna, the woman sitting beside her, comfortable from the start. They found connection immediately when Moxie realized who Johanna was.

"Oh, for heaven's sake!" said Moxie in sudden recognition of the woman's name. "Attorney Loyal Roberts said you have vast knowledge of setting up non-profits and will help steer me in fulfilling my friends' requests."

"Yes. I am the business consultant Eunice and Mildred have arranged for you to work with. Oh, what dear-hearted and well-meaning women those two were. I'll miss them both enormously.

We've been working together on different entrepreneurial projects, or social enterprises, as Miss Eunice liked to call them for a long time."

"Well, it's nice to put a face with the name," said Moxie, no longer feeling pushed into something she was not ready for.

Just then Matt walked over and greeted the wild-haired woman by name.

"Oh, so Matt, you already know Johanna."

"Yes! She's been working with me on a project."

Suddenly conversation was interrupted when a man came to the podium. "If everyone would take their seats I'd like to start right away." Everyone became quiet in the room.

The evenings agenda was read and #1 was quickly addressed. Each item was quickly ticked off the list. Moxie couldn't help but feel the commitment and cohesiveness among the members of NNN in the room. There were some stumbling blocks, but some innovative thinking, as well as some giving and taking of ideas which smoothed things over.

When the meeting was adjourned Johanna rose from her seat. "See, that's what l like about working with people in this community. Their approach to ironing out problems is refreshing."

Matt agreed. "Take the idea of starting a Community Sponsored Garden. It makes so much sense for *the Way to the Heart Is through the Garden* to spearhead the project. And a joint effort of all our NNN members personally canvassing each business for volunteers to plant and maintain the community garden seems like a slam dunk to me. It's something I wouldn't mind getting involved with."

Johanna rose from her seat. "Moxie, it's great to meet you. I need to head home, but I'll see both of you soon. Look forward to it."

That night Moxie slept like a baby feeling as if whatever it was that was on the horizon, she was in good hands and being looked out for, thank the Lord.

Chapter 5

ANOTHER FULL BOX, Moxie said to herself. She didn't know where she was moving to, but a relocation was certain unless there was some unpredictable occurrence preventing it. Once Beverly, the sewing shop manager, had signed the sales agreement and paid a sizable deposit, Moxie felt confident enough to pack up even more. Her personal items were only a small part of the overall task. For years Moxie had been traipsing around with few belongings, that is until the two old women, her dear friends, began passing along their sewing supplies, jewelry and anything they thought Moxie might like or could use. Moxie loved some of the cool stuff they passed along to her for repurposing.

Since her large apartment over the sewing shop served as personal living space and her sewing studio, the big challenge would come with packing up all her sewing supplies and fabrics. She'd been making curtains, drapes, cushion covers, table linens and such for commercial clients. The fabrics were heavy and cumbersome to move. She kept dragging her feet on packing up the studio. When had her full steam ahead attitude disappeared?

The day she made the definitive decision to make a break from Hopewell and move to Belle Aire, she felt freedom like she'd never felt before. Perhaps because Eunice's words came to her out of the blue just before making the big decision. She'd actually listened! "Moxie," Miss Eunice said to her one time when she was feeling particularly anxious about her life's direction, "sometimes you just gotta let go and let God." Wow, what a difference that had made in reducing her stress level.

Just as Moxie decided to call it a day and stop packing, the phone rang. She picked up the call right away.

"So, how is it going over there?"

"Oh fine, oh fine..."

"Moxie, I think I know you well enough to know something is bothering you. Fess up."

"Well, packing the sewing stuff all seems so overwhelming, Matt. Even though I am only moving a few towns away and not across country it still needs to be done. At this point sounds like it's gonna be only a temporary move, so I dread the thought of hauling it twice."

"Moxie, don't think like that! Positive vibes and energy only. When the doubts come, just kick 'em to the curb. Anything is possible when...hey, would it lighten the burden if I said when you're ready to pack up the heavy fabrics, I'll come help?"

"Oh Matt, you don't have to do that."

"Don't look a gift horse in the mouth. Besides how hard could it be to fold up the fabrics not on bolts. I bet I could do it as well as anyone else."

"I suppose." When she thought about the razor-sharp creases he always had in his khaki pants and the carefully ironed box pleats on the back of his oxford shirts, why wouldn't she let him fold reams of fabric taken off their bolts?

"Now, where will I be moving your studio supplies once they're all packed up, downstairs?"

"Ummm, that's part of the puzzle I haven't solved. They don't want it downstairs. They are discontinuing all lines of upholstery fabrics since I'm not going to handle the commercial accounts. You haven't forgotten, have you? You are supposed to be helping me find a place to go Mr. Realtor."

"Doesn't that make things easier knowing you'll be making a clean break from the business?"

"Well, I wouldn't say a completely clean break."

"I don't understand. It's a nearly a done deal.

You'll have no control over what the shop does since they are buying you out lock, stock and barrel."

"Matt it's not that easy. I may want to include them in my next step. It's hard to completely let go of something you love."

"Moxie, what are you withholding from me?"

"Nothing intentionally. Matt, how can I know what the next step will be when I don't even know where I'm going?"

"I gotta go Moxie, duty is calling. All I ask is that you keep an open mind and heart. Will you?"

"Ok. I will."

"Things will work out. Johanna is going to help you with that."

"Promise me you'll stop fretting?" Moxie rolled her eyes knowing Matt couldn't see her.

"Ok. I promise!"

"Was your hand on the Bible?"

"Matt! Stop! I get it, ok? I've handed it over."

Chapter 6

"I'VE GOT NO TIME TO WASTE," Matt said, as he stood in front of Johanna the business consultant he had been working with.

"I'm afraid we're losing Moxie. I don't understand. Last week she was so fired up about her new stomping grounds and now, well, the doubts are creeping in to put it mildly."

"It happens, bro."

"Oh, believe me I know!"

"Matt, leave it to me. I've got a plan of action."

"Do you? Ok, then. I'm depending on you to keep her fired up. If only word would come through."

A few minutes later Johanna was on the phone with Moxie.

"Moxie, how are you? I really enjoyed meeting you last week. Sorry our time was so limited with the meeting and all. How's your free time these days?"

"Non-existent."

"I'd like to be your emissary of sorts and spend a few days with you so you can become better acquainted with your new community."

"Oh, I don't know, Johanna." Moxie thought about it for a few minutes. "Well, ok, maybe it's what I need."

"Tell you what, how about Monday, that will give you four days so you can continue what you are doing. I'll pick you up at 9 a.m. How's that? Too early?"

"No, no. That's fine. Sounds like a plan. Johanna, thanks!"

Four days later Moxie was roused by a loud knock. She jumped up out of bed, threw on her robe, opened the door and there was Johanna standing there looking all bright-eyed. Moxie rubbed the sleep out of her eyes.

"Well, good morning, Sunshine! Are you ready for your day to begin?" Johanna looked Moxie up and down wondering why she had on her robe and pajamas.

"What time is it?" Moxie asked, squinting into the bright morning light.

"It's 9 o'clock.

"What! I don't know the last time I slept in so late. Wow! I must have been tired."

"I have strict instructions for today. The girls

down at the shop have told me I am supposed to hijack you all day long. I can't let you anywhere near here until 5 p.m. It's a day for R & R whether you like it or not. Those are the orders."

"I had my R & R for the week. Remember? At the park on Saturday with you! We meditated and stretched, remember? Or are you still zoned out?"

"Did you enjoy it?"

"Actually, despite the trouble I had staying in 'the zone' I did enjoy the new experience. Johanna, thanks."

"A half an hour meditation and stretch, that's really not your definition of R & R, is it? A half an hour? Girlfriend, I am going to teach you something about chillaxing beyond meditation."

"What's that? Chillaxin."

"What do you mean what's that? You know. We are going to chill, vegetate, decompress."

"Oh, you mean goof-off? Johanna, you don't know much about me. I've been hanging around two eighty-year-old women, let me rephrase that – two firecracker eighty-something women who had more energy than I could keep up with. But, their lingo hadn't yet been brought current. When we hung out together, we goofed off!"

"Gotcha! Now throw on some clothes. I am taking you to get the best cup of jitter juice you have ever had in your life."

"Jitter juice? Well, yeah, that's what my daughter calls it. I call it java."

"You have a daughter?"

"Of course, I have a daughter. I didn't get these gray hairs creeping in from nothing!" Moxie had been wondering how old Johanna was because of her head full of grays.

"Can I shower first?"

Johanna looked at the clock on her cell phone. "Nope. Why bother? After we grab a cup of joe we are headed for the spa – full treatment head to toe. You'll be rubbed down and smacked around 'til that body of yours glows like nobody's business. Then you'll get your shower. You'll be all spiffy for the next thing on today's list."

"List? I thought we are going to chillax! What if I don't want to be rubbed down and smacked around?" Moxie had no idea what that meant in the context of a spa experience. She'd never had one before.

"Oh, stop! Don't be such a stick in the mud now – you'll get a mud treatment later when we get to the spa!"

"Johanna, what in the world did you take before you came over here anyway? What's gotten into you? How many cups of jitter juice have you had already? You are hardly the goddess of serenity this morning."

"Let's go, darlin' we haven't got all day. Time's a wastin'."

Moxie ran to her bedroom, threw on her favorite pair of jeans and light-weight cotton sweater, quickly brushed her hair and grabbed her purse and returned to where Johanna was standing.

"Nope! Put it down."

"Put what down?"

"Your purse and cellphone. They are not invited to come along."

"But...I need them."

"Why?"

"Because I've got important stuff in them...you know, that says who I am. My driver's license and such."

"Girlfriend, by the time I'm done with you, you won't know who you are anyway. You'll be a new person." Moxie continued toward the door with her purse in hand.

"Nope. No need for either one of them." Moxie was too tired already to argue. Maybe this wasn't a good match with a business consultant after all. But, despite her doubts, she left her purse and cellphone behind and followed Johanna's lead. Out the door she went.

"Here we are in Belle Aire! The Steam Room is just around the corner."

"Hey, are you messin' with me? You said we

were going to get coffee first. I need that!" Moxie was surprised at her own boldness. Taking up for herself like that.

Johanna hustled Moxie out of the car, the whole time Moxie stated her objections about going to the "Steam Room" first, thinking it was a sauna at a spa.

"Trust me. We will get you your coffee. Follow me!"

Johanna led the way and opened the door to the place. The two women walked into the coffee joint the likes of which Moxie had never seen before.

Moxie looked around. "Wow – I had no idea a place like this exists! I am used to going to the Open Doors Soup and Sandwich Shop over by the park in Hopewell with Mildred."

The two women grabbed a high-top table, and a waitress came over to where they were sitting.

"Hi Johanna! What will it be today? Cappuccino, Tazo, Expresso, Café Misto? You name it we have it."

What the heck kind of language is that? Moxie thought.

Johanna turned to Moxie. "So, girl, what are you thinkin'? How would you like to start your morning?"

"Do you want me to be honest? I'm thinking

I am feeling intimidated. I am used to a mug of basic black coffee period. End of sentence."

"Well, girl, today is a new day – you're gonna start livin! How about I order for you?"

"That'd be great. I have no idea what any of it is anyway so what's the difference?".

"Oh girl...we've got a long way to go, then."

Johanna placed the order for something Moxie didn't recognize. While they waited for their order, Moxie made small talk about her observances about the coffee shop. To her the equipment to make a cup of coffee looked like the space station of the future compared to the stove top percolator she inherited from Eunice's rental apartment. Moxie watched the stainless-steel machines grinding beans, brewing them and steaming and frothing milk, and thought, *Gee whiz! All this luxury for a dang cup of coffee?*

The waitress returned with a tray and set Johanna's cup down in front of her stating what it was. Then she put Moxie's in front of her, again, stating what it was. Moxie inhaled the aromas wafting out of her cup. It smelled like dessert of some kind. She looked at it and thought about the unique mug. Nothing like the standard white diner mug she was used to. The foam on the top of the steaming liquid formed a heart shape.

"Well, girl – what are you gonna do, sit there all day and look at it? Taste it!"

"Johanna, please," Moxie said, lowering her voice to a whisper. "I feel like I woke up on the wrong side of the bed. Calling me 'girl' is making me feel cranky! My name is Moxie."

"Moxie, I am so sorry. I am glad you are living up to your name and having the nerve to tell me to cool it. Maybe I am coming on a little too strong. I just want you to enjoy this day we have planned for you."

Moxie didn't know who "we" was, as far as she could tell there was only one person sitting across from her at the table. Moxie lifted her cup and slowly took a sip.

"Wow – is that ever good! What is it again?" Johanna proceeded to tell her.

I'll be right back. I need to visit the lady's room I haven't been since I woke up. We rushed out of the house so quickly. Moxie went and did her business and returned.

"I ordered you a bite to eat. Hope that's ok. I figured our spa treatments will take a few hours and we can't last that long without any food in our bellies."

A few hours at the spa? Seemed like a wasted few hours to Moxie, but she reminded herself not to be critical and keep her mouth shut. "So, what did you order me for food?"

"I ordered both of us the same thing. Avocado toast, veggie scramble with a side of fresh fruit.

Avocado toast? Moxie couldn't remember ever having that before and she imagined the veggie scramble to be scrambled eggs with an onion or perhaps a green pepper thrown in like on the menu at the Open Doors Soup and Sandwich Shop, but surely it would come with a much higher price tag. Moxie always had a craving for fruit, so she knew she'd at least recognize that.

"Sounds good, Johanna."

The girls continued making small talk as they waited for the food to arrive.

"Here we go, here's your breakfast." The waitress set square white plates down with artfully arranged food. It looked so appetizing. Beautiful, really.

"We probably shouldn't dawdle too long. We don't want to miss our spa treatments." The women dug in and ate. When Moxie finished it all, she stretched, rubbing her stomach.

"Wow, that was great. The avocado toast was yummy! And the fruit bowl. What was in it?"

"That would be mango, star fruit, paw-paw and papaya, kiwi and kumquat."

"It sure tasted good." Moxie asked because she didn't recognize any of it. It sure looked different than the square diced-up canned fruit salad they served at Open Doors Soup and Sandwich Shop.

"All exotics. Glad you liked it."

The waitress came over and bid them good-bye. Moxie and Johanna walked out of the restaurant and Moxie looked up at the sign over the door. *Now*, Moxie thought, *I've got the steam to face whatever comes next.* As they climbed into the car, Moxie realized something. Neither one of them had paid.

"Wait, we can't just drive off like this, Johanna. We didn't pay."

Johanna waved her hands, "We've been taken care of. No worries!"

Moxie looked out the window as they drove along Commerce Street. She was surprised when Johanna took a right turn onto High Street because she knew where the health spa was in Belle Aire, she'd seen it in passing. Johanna sped right past the building and kept on going. At the risk of seeming like a backseat driver, Moxie spoke up anyway.

"You just passed the spa, Johanna."

"Oh, that's not the one we are going to. We are going to the Wellness Resort outside of town. Moxie sat quietly enjoying the ride. Most of her travel until recently had been on foot or when she hitched a ride with Eunice or Mildred. They ordinarily tended to not veer off the beaten path. Moxie was seeing all kinds of places she never knew existed, including the dirt road they were traveling.

"Tell me, are we still in Belle Aire?"

"Yes, the town line extends further than you might imagine."

Finally, when they were about 5 miles from the center of town, they came to a sign Merciful Touch: A Wellness Resort. Johanna turned in and headed down a long driveway. They parked and got out of the car. Had Moxie not been with her new friend, she wasn't sure she'd have ventured down the long driveway in an isolated location. Although in every other way, the place looked very respectable. "A high-end structure with high-end finishes," as Mildred would have described the building. Although larger, not too different in style from Mildred's home.

As soon as the women opened the door, they were greeted by a little ankle biter. But the dog was hardly that. She sweetly came and sniffed Moxie and Johanna when they bent down to pet her. Satisfied they met with her approval, she climbed into her dog bed and settled.

"Welcome Johanna! I am delighted to have you back." The two exchanged a few more niceties.

"And who is your friend?" The woman had a soft melodious voice and she seemed to have appeared out of nowhere.

"This is Moxie. Moxie meet Amity." Moxie extended her hand and was struck immediately by the woman's soft touch. She wore a long, off-white gauzy, flowy dress with monotone off-white embroidery scrolling down the front placket. Her feet were clad in flat, strappy sandals.

"Well, I'll be with you today, Moxie. And Johanna, we have you scheduled with Galen."

She pulled out a clipboard from behind the front desk. "Let's see what we have you scheduled for – The Full Service – Luxury Package, which means – Chakra Clearing, Detoxifying Body Cleanse, Sulphur Soak, Massage, Hot Rocks, The 24 Gold Karat Facial Mask and the All-Body Mud Treatment. That's not necessarily in the right order. Throughout your day we will fit in each of these treatments. As always, there are light, healthy snacks such as fresh fruit, nuts and yoghurt and all kinds of drinks available. Speak up if you need it. Remember, it's particularly important that you stay hydrated."

"My word! I'm not sure I need...I haven't a clue what all those treatments mean." Moxie said as she began to raise objections.

Johanna reached out and touched Moxie's

wrist as if in a kind gesture. "Moxie," the tone in her voice was as warm as her gesture, "the words of the day are lean into it, acquiesce, go with the flow!"

"Well, let's get started," said Amity with a broad smile directed at Johanna, as if to indicate a "thank you for helping me out." She led them further into the building. "Say goodbye, Moxie. You'll see your friend, Johanna at the end of the treatments."

"Moxie, I promise you will feel like a new person. Both of us will. Bye, Moxie. Enjoy! And remember, just go with the flow!"

At first, Moxie was very self-conscious and felt a lot of resistance both in her body and her spirit. She wondered if Amity noticed. Amity said many carefully measured words that she hoped would make Moxie feel safe and open to each new experience. As Moxie began to trust, and as they moved from treatment to treatment, she let down her guard, relaxed her muscles and soaked it all up, nearly nodding off during the massage.

When the treatment was all over and both women had showered, they met back up. Moxie wanted to gush. There were so many feelings and emotions she had about the luxury spa treatment.

Johanna and Moxie said their goodbyes to Amity and Galen, the two spa attendants, walked out and got in the car. Johanna asked Moxie to sum up the experience in one sentence. Moxie responded, "It was a complete and total enlightenment experience." Johanna was aware that it would take Moxie time to internally process the wellness spa experience since she was new to it.

As they headed down the road, Moxie sat quietly beginning to do just that – think about what she had just experienced. She enjoyed every step but at times she felt uncomfortable, mostly because she was not used to doing something so completely self-indulgent. And as naïve as she was, Moxie had no idea others allowed themselves such luxuries either. She didn't tell Johanna she'd never even had a manicure or pedicure before for fear Johanna would add more indulgences to the day's services. In her book, Moxie considered the treatments they'd just gotten, over-the-top. It wasn't a thought she'd ever share with Johanna for fear of hurting her feelings.

"Everyone has their own standards of what they need to make themselves feel validated," Eunice often said to Moxie. "Many people work so hard with a specific goal in mind of someday being able to enjoy the best of the best. If that's what they need to make themselves feel whole and complete, so be it. It's not ours to judge."

Johanna pulled over to the side of the road to grab a piece of paper from her purse. "Let's see here what is next on the list. Oh crap! It's in the other direction." She looked at her clock on her cell phone.

"My word, its already 4 p.m. and there is so much more on our list of things to do and see."

"There is more on the list? What is it?"

"Moxie, I am not going to tell you and be the spoiler. But there's no way we can get to much more today. Many places close at 5 p.m. The spa treatment took much longer than I anticipated."

Yeah, all day, thought Moxie. But not wanting to appear unappreciative, Moxie didn't say exactly what she was thinking.

"Look, Johanna, can we call it a day? The spa treatment was so beautifully luxurious, I just want to go home and soak in the experience some more. You know, while my muscles are relaxed let them stay that way and enjoy the euphoric feeling."

"Actually, that sounds like a good idea. Let's plan on another outing in a few days. Going home and crashing sounds really good to me, too."

"It's a deal. Just say when, Johanna, and I will be ready for our next adventure."

"Let's see. How about Friday?"

"Perfect."

"Oh, the girls at the sewing shop aren't gonna like me bringing you back early. We'll have to sneak. And promise me you won't go down to the shop 'til tomorrow."

Moxie promised and got out of the car quietly and quietly tiptoed up the back stairs to her apartment.

Sleep came early that night. Moxie couldn't wait 'til Friday. If it was going to be anything like today's experience, she was psyched.

Chapter 7

"MATT, SLOW DOWN, you're driving too fast. You don't want another headline in the paper like Eunice and Mildred's, do you? Only this time it will read 'Second Joy Ride Casualty in Hopewell.' What's with you anyway?"

"I'm feeling like a pressure cooker only it's in my office rather than in the kitchen. I'm being nagged by the bane of my existence right now, finding a place to live.

"What? For me or you?"

"Both!"

"Both?"

"I've never discussed it before but I'm like you, I am now an orphan, too. My parents passed a few years ago." He was talking as fast as he was driving.

"I wondered why you hadn't mentioned them. In the donut shop you talked about them frequently. So, they passed during the years when you and I were out of touch?"

"Yep. And, well let's just say I've been left in a position something like you. But what's different is I've got six women nagging at me because I've been dragging my feet on the last item on my list as executor and man of the house. They want things wrapped up, and so do I."

"Misery loves company."

Matt didn't respond. He didn't want to tip Moxie off about what he had been thinking. No, not until all the ducks were in a row. He couldn't risk Moxie's feet getting any colder.

"So, where are you going with this, Matt?"

Matt inhaled and decided he'd be brave and reveal just a little. "Hopefully back to the kitchen."

"Back to the kitchen? Surely you don't mean back to making donuts!"

"Not quite."

"Well, what about real estate, Matt? Seems to me you've done quite well for yourself."

"Hmmmm."

"Moxie, promise me you will not say a word. Not to anyone. Can I trust you? I have great faith you can keep a secret."

"I can."

"Even with all those cacklin' hens down in the

sewing shop? I know women, Moxie. Remember, I'm in the middle of six sisters."

"I promise, Girl Scouts honor!"

"Yea, right. You told me a long, long time ago you were never a Girl Scout or a whatever they called the little ones...Brownies. You said, you regretted not being able to sell Girl Scout cookies. It always looked like fun."

"I told you that?"

"Yeah. The day I interviewed you to work at the donut shop."

"Must have been really stressed. I don't remember. What did that have to do with getting a job at a donut shop?"

Matt shrugged his shoulders.

"Anyway, I will promise to keep my trap shut. I don't want to ruin anything you've got cooking."

Matt drove along silently.

"So, you gonna tell me or not?"

Matt inhaled again and then paused. "The real estate business no longer aligns with my values and I've made some realizations."

"Like?"

"Making lots of money over doing what I love isn't worth it. I've been kinda miserable. Lesson realized. I miss the creativity of being in the kitchen."

"Again. I must ask. Cooking donuts?"

"No...No. Moxie we were out of touch for some years. Since then, I've really expanded my cookin' repertoire. I even took culinary classes."

That's not all, Moxie thought as she looked at him wearing a tie. With his neatly cut and combed hair, his appearance was quite different than the days of standing over the fry cooker, the hot grease vat, plopping in "O" shaped raw dough.

Moxie made a sudden realization. "But Matt! What's going to happen with finding me a place to live?"

"I have no intention of leaving you hanging! Trust me."

"Well, I've heard that many times in my life," said Moxie. "From a whole string of 'uneven mothers' as Mildred so delicately put it."

"I'm sorry. But I'm not one of them."

"True enough."

"Moxie, that's all I can say for now!"

"See that? You're already keeping me hanging!"

"No, Moxie. I promise you. See, I'm working on a few things and there are both privacy issues and zoning issues. I will tell you more when I can. So, are we done with our joy ride?"

"Yeah, I guess so. You can take me home, Matt."

Matt soon steered into to the parking lot behind the sewing shop. They sat quietly for a few moments.

"Moxie, you and I, we do all right together, don't you think?"

"I guess. I mean yeah, I guess so."

Moxie opened her door. Matt opened his and hustled around to help Moxie out of her seat. She stepped out of the car a bit perplexed wondering why Matt would ask her such a question.

"Bye, Matt. Thanks for the ride."

He promised her again he wouldn't leave her hanging.

That evening Moxie decided at some point, yes, she did need to learn to trust, and the time was now. She liked Matt right from the get-go as a boss. And perhaps his firing of her had more to do with her than him. To be honest with herself she wasn't exactly the model employee. Neither trustworthy nor dependable back then. *Thank the Lord, I grew up*, she thought.

"Moxie," Matt said one day to her surprise, "I can't help but notice what a professional you've become." That felt good. What better validation could she have received since Mildred and Eunice had echoed the same thoughts.

Moxie had worked hard. But it was Eunice and Mildred's words that had really made a difference. When they invited Moxie into a three-way partnership, each told Moxie they felt something was beginning to unfold for the future of their business. "God has a bigger plan for us than we have for ourselves," said Mildred.

Yet, Moxie thought, *still, sometimes I question.*

Chapter 8

THE CORNERS OF HER MOUTH turned up in a smile as Moxie slipped the sweatshirt Eunice had given her one Christmas over her head. She read what was scrawled across her chest. "*When life gives you scraps, make a quilt and fill it with batting.*"

She worked hard for a few hours packing until 9 a.m. when it was time to call it quits, shower and change into something more presentable for her day out with Johanna. She looked forward to her second outing with her Belle Aire tour guide, Johanna.

Johanna arrived promptly at ten, and after seeing what she wore, Moxie was glad she'd chosen to dress in one of her newer outfits. Johanna liked her outfit and said so. "Aren't you the picture of fashion this morning? Your jeans fit you to a tee and that smart looking floral peplum top nicely accentuates your pretty figure. The orange shoes...

well, they're the cat's meow. Between the shoes and that top you look like a pert poppy. The short fluttery sleeves look like a poppy's tissue paper petals waving in the breeze. Let's go!"

Moxie locked the apartment door and the two women got in the car and off they went.

"Where are we going?" asked Moxie.

"You'll see."

"Hey, I wanted to thank you for the other day at the spa. After what I experienced how could I ever continue living the same way? I truly felt like a new person." Later that evening after her spa treatment, Moxie ran across the street to the store and sprang for a San Pellegrino instead of a sugary Sprite. She decided right there and then she was going to begin to live life differently and allow herself a few more luxuries.

"Well, we are just getting started my friend. Moxie you really have lived a sheltered life, haven't you?"

"Well," Moxie said, taking up for herself, "over the past five years I've spent nearly every waking moment between three places, if that's what you mean. If I wasn't at Eunice's, I was at Mildred's, and if I wasn't there, I was at Sew the Heart. The three of us were all wrapped up in trying to bring the business current and train employees about new ways of doing business. Most of it was up to me because they knew nothing about technology, keeping inventory in the computer and integrating a Point-of-Sale system. Before I started working there, the place was being run like something from the dinosaur age using a cash register from 1800 and a tablet of paper receipts and an abacus." Johanna laughed.

"No, really! Now we have nearly a turn-key operation. Just imagine if I really knew what I was doing."

"Oh, stop that! Apparently, you did know what you were doing! You don't have to answer if you don't want to, but do you think your two friends would be happy about your decision to sell?

Moxie didn't answer.

"Go ahead, Moxie, you can say it. It's none of your beeswax, Johanna."

"It's none of your beeswax, Johanna."

"Good girl, Moxie! No offense taken. I know you're a smart girl with a voice of her own!"

Moxie laughed. She was really beginning to enjoy this new friendship with Johanna and feeling okay about not doing things just to please others. As they drove along, Moxie pondered how comfortable she felt with her decision. Deep down she felt Mildred and Eunice really did want Moxie to find a life that suited her wants and not theirs. There was a whole new world out there just waiting to be explored. And Moxie was determined to go after it.

As they drove into the historic downtown, once again Moxie was charmed by what she saw. As the car zipped along, Moxie marveled at the well-kept businesses and how free of trash the streets were in the historic Main Street district. The surrounding homes were every bit as lovely with a mixture of architectural styles from charming bungalows with a cottagey look, to Victorians with turrets and gingerbread trim, to clean farmhouse style, to nice cookie cutter homes in well-kept community developments.

"So, Johanna, you're planning to stay in the downtown area today?" She nodded yes.

"Oh good! I'm so curious to know more about this place I'm moving to. Will we have time to walk the streets?"

"Sure. I am going to take you first to the far end of the village." As Johanna drove, Moxie continued to be drawn in by what she was seeing. "Here we are!"

Moxie looked at a sprawling Victorian house in front of her which was surrounded by an old black wrought iron fence containing the most beautiful gardens Moxie had ever seen in her life."

"This just takes my breath away, Johanna, and I haven't even been inside yet!" Moxie looked up at the sign on the building. "The Way to the Heart Is through the Garden." *Ah*, thought Moxie, *this is the business that will be spearheading the developing CSA.*

"Girl, you ain't seen nothin' yet!" After she said it, Johanna regretted it. The other day Moxie made it clear she didn't take a liking to be calling "girl." Perhaps in her previous life someone had called her that in a demeaning way. Johanna only talked like that to girlfriends whom she liked to spend time with and kid around with. It was not meant as an insult or to be degrading.

The two women got out of Johanna's bright yellow Mini-Cooper convertible which was about the coolest car Moxie had ever been in. The first time Moxie sat in it she couldn't help but contrast it to the pink Cadillac from days long gone by that she had been riding around in with Eunice and Mildred. As embarrassing as riding in a pink Cadillac was, Eunice helped get her to and from. Now, it was as if she was being transported by a busy little bee flitting here and there rather than by a vehicle usually driven by vintage top-selling Avon ladies of star status. *God bless them and the life they gave me*, thought Moxie. How she missed them.

Johanna led Moxie down the flagstone walkway

toward the front door of the place. The stone path kept the flowers somewhat at bay. They were greeted by a woman with a straw, broad-brimmed garden hat, garden gloves and a sturdy green apron which had the name of the business embroidered across the front of it. "Hi, Johanna! It's been a while since we've seen one another! How are you?"

Moxie stood quietly and listened to the two women wondering whether there was a soul in town Johanna didn't know.

"And who is your friend?"

"This is Moxie, she's moving to town, and I'm getting her acquainted with everything and everyone."

"Oh, Moxie! Hello. I am Heather. I am sorry about the sad accident I read about in the newspaper. It was as if Heather was expecting her. It was the first encounter Moxie had out and about where the loss of Eunice and Mildred was mentioned. Moxie became very misty-eyed, so she reached down and swiped at her shin as if shoeing a pest away."

When she stood from her bent position, she had gathered herself. "So, you knew Eunice and Mildred, did you?"

"Oh, everyone knew Mildred and Eunice. Seems they had their hands in everything in this town. But I didn't personally know them, if you know what I mean."

"They certainly left their mark. In fact, more than they will ever know," Moxie said. The three women chuckled.

"Indeed, they did!" said Heather. "But Johanna knows more about them than I ever did."

Johanna smiled.

"Well! Come on in!" Heather said, gesturing them forward. "I'll give you a full tour. Where would you like to start?"

"Heather, it is a beautiful day, isn't it? Are you all set up to serve lunch outdoors this early in the spring?"

"Yes, you've lucked out! This will be our first day of plein-air dining!"

"Then let's start inside. That will bide us some time until the Garden Café opens. Johanna looked at the time on her cellphone. "We've got a while yet! After our inside tour, Moxie can tour the outbuildings and exterior gardens while we are waiting for lunch to be served."

"Come on ladies, let's go!" She walked forward with Moxie and Johanna trailing behind. It was then that Moxie saw the sentiment on the back of Heather's long-sleeved tee-shirt. "*Where flowers bloom, so does hope.*" ~ Lady Bird Johnson.

They were led to a window-seat in the building

flanked on each end by bookshelves filled with garden books. Moxie quickly perused the titles.

"What a wide range of books you have related to gardening, botanicals, herbs, garden design, garden wisdom, birding and more!" A few display tables beautifully arranged with books and other garden gewgaws and a few easy chairs for people to sit and enjoy made the area hospitable.

It was a delightful space. Only thing Moxie saw missing was a woodstove where people could gather like in the old times for community and garden talk during the cold off-season.

"If it wasn't for the rest of the shop which I am dying to see, I'd plant myself right here, make myself comfortable and grow roots, right here!" Heather and Johanna laughed when Moxie said it.

"I know, right?" piped up Johanna.

"Excuse the faded cushion on the window seat. We are a little shabby chic around here." Moxie thought that was part of the charm. "Besides with the sun coming in the bay window, we have to have the cushion recovered every couple of years."

"I know someone who might be able to do that for you. Perhaps Sunbrella™ fabric might work well there." Moxie grabbed a business card out of her back pocket and handed it to Heather.

The women moved on toward the back of the

building. "Most of the stuff in this room will be taken out outside next week, but for now, it's inside. Any type of hardscape that could be brought indoors for the winter is in here," explained Heather. What Moxie was seeing was interesting. Other than Mildred's talk about her damask roses and the small terrarium Eunice have given her, Moxie knew not a thing about gardening.

"These things give me the creepy crawlies," Moxie said steering clear of the concrete gargoyles. She walked directly to the garden angels, and stood there quietly, almost reverently looking down at the garden statuary surrounding her. One corner of the room was filled with bird seed galore and unique birdfeeders unlike any she'd seen before.

How cool! Moxie thought when she saw the birdhouses made from dried gourds. Once settled she'd come back and treat herself to one. But first, she needed to find a place to nest of her own.

The three women moved into a large room where there was a woman setting up for something. "This is our classroom space where we teach flower arranging and floral design. Tamsin is setting up for a lesson this afternoon. Oh, her arrangements are literally to die for. Something very special! She's full of the English gardening blood and we are very fortunate to have her on staff. She's done arrangements for some pretty impressive mansion houses in England."

"After Eunice and Mildred passed, I came home to the most incredible bouquet of flowers unlike any I have ever seen in my life," said Moxie. "They were sitting on my doorstep. What a surprise! There was nothing to indicate who they were from other than a small blank card with the name of this garden center. Tamsin, could the arrangement have been your creation? And would you know who they may have been from?"

"You know the old adage about being given a gift, don't you?" asked Tamsin.

"Well...no."

"When given a gift, accept it to honor the giver. Sounds to me like it was meant to be a delivery from an anonymous admirer."

"Thank you, Tamsin. I will remember that. And it was a wonderful teaser to get me to come see what the The Way to the Heart Is Through the Garden is all about."

"Now," said Heather, "this leads us directly into the floral shop where we do all our incoming orders for flower arrangements." Moxie looked around and was positively overwhelmed by the refreshing smells of greenery. It was like walking into Santa's workshop! Women were all a buzz with activity. "We are especially busy in here today.

The B & B down the street has an elite corporate retreat arriving this week and have ordered fresh flowers every day for each bedroom and for their common areas and dining room. We've had a wonderful time consulting with them because as you may or may not know, each flower and each color that goes into an arrangement has specific significance. Their goals for their conference are being displayed in their floral choices. We appreciate their business."

Moxie didn't want to nose into who their corporate client was, but she couldn't help but wonder if they were into matchmaking. Years ago, old Miss Mildred told Moxie about how Victorian ladies selected flowers for nosegays and floral arrangements for very sentimental reasons. "Flowers," she said, "spoke a language of their own."

As they moved to the next area, Moxie noted how truly fitting the name of garden center was. *One does have to see this place to fully experience it*, she thought.

"One more room and then we will head outside to where we have more garden hardscape, such exterior statuaries and pavers, that are too large to be brought indoors for the winter. Then we will take a quick glance into the tool shed, the barn with all the plant food and nutrients. You'll love the water garden area. Finally, into the greenhouses we will go where you will see all kinds of things growing - exotics, houseplants, topiaries, cacti and bonsai plants for little fairy gardens. The perennials and annuals in pots everywhere outside, all surrounding the house are sold to our customers to take home for planting."

"I feel like I am walking through a fairytale this morning. My goodness, Heather, does this fantasy story ever end?" asked Moxie.

"Actually, it doesn't. If we in the NNN are doing our jobs right, and working on our mission, the story should keep growing! But we can't get into that right now. Don't miss this, Moxie. Step inside the last room in this building."

A woman with wild frizzy hair something like Johanna's, but the color of a newly minted copper penny, appeared from behind an area of drying flowers hanging from the ceiling. She was clad in a long flowing sage-colored linen dress, bedecked and bedazzled with complimentary colored crystals and beads hanging around her neck and dangling from her ears. Her long ginger tresses were held back from her face with a hair comb shaped like a butterfly. The way the monarch was positioned it looked like it had just alit on the side of her head.

"Welcome to my haven. My name is Helena, and I am the herbalist here. This is where we take flowers and herbs from the heart of our garden, dry them and then use the petals, the essential oils, and the rest of the plant material for all kinds of products for kitchen, bath and household. When you go through the village and beyond, you'll begin to see a trail of our products because 'alone we can do so little but together we can do so much.'" Helena then pointed out some of the flower and herbs which hung from the rafters and their specific uses. The odors in the room were nearly overwhelming.

When Helena finished explaining her part in the operations at the garden center, Heather spoke up. "We are not done yet. Let's head out of the building and into the other areas we spoke about."

"Heather, if I am not saying much, don't think I am not interested! I am trying to soak all this up! Absorb all I can about this enterprise. Are you the owner?"

"Let's just say I have a large interest. Without the wonderful staff and the NNN partners we've been blessed with, this center wouldn't be thriving like it is. We took this place and revived the business. It was ready to meet its demise. The importance of our employees and partners-at-large such as Johanna and her tribe must not be understated.

Each one of them, their hearts are deeply in it. That's what is bringing success."

Moxie became even more eager to become part of what was happening in town. What a groundswell of activity here. It buoyed her to think this was going to be her new community.

Heather kept her promise, and they took a quick tour of every area she had previously mentioned. Moving from area to area, Moxie couldn't believe gardening involved so much more than a pot of red geraniums. Yes, she lived a sheltered existence alright. The day was still nearly in its dawn, and Moxie felt as if she was experiencing an alternate world experience.

Near the greenhouse Moxie smelled an odor which she couldn't put her finger on. "What is that I am smelling?" she asked. Outside the entrance of the green house there was a shoulder high potted plant growing into a large heart shape."

"You're smelling rosemary." Heather pointed to the plant. "When the sun is on it, it's especially pungent." Heather broke off a piece crushed it and brought her hands up to Moxie's nose. Moxie inhaled.

"Now you'll remember the scent of rosemary."

"Does it grow like that?"

"Like what, Moxie?"

"In a heart shape."

"Oh no," Heather laughed. "The herb needs to be trained, trimmed, loved and nearly teased into a topiary growing like that."

"Kind of like how I am getting you to grow!" said Johanna, smiling at Moxie. She reached over and gave Moxie a chin up motion with her index finger.

"Hey! There's some truth to that!" Moxie elbowed her newly found friend's rib in a friendly gesture.

"Quit it, that hurts!" Johanna said rubbing her side, laughing.

As soon as they walked into the greenhouse there were terrariums and other miniature plants. They reminded Moxie of her own succulents that she had planted in the cavity of Miss Eunice's old typewriter. The succulents had given her much joy and she appreciated their non-demanding nature. Moxie wondered if this shop was where Eunice had purchased her terrarium. She made a mental note to consider buying a topiary in the future. Moxie knew this place would be one of her favorite stomping grounds. It had found its way into her heart. Her interest in plants was growing.

When the green house tour was over, Johanna looked at the clock on her cellphone. "The Garden Café opens at 11:30 a.m., doesn't it, Heather?"

"Yes."

"Moxie, are you up for an early lunch?"

"Yes, I didn't have much for breakfast. This tour has been fabulous. I've worked up an appetite in more ways than one!"

"Heather, would you like to join us for lunch? My treat."

"I don't mean to be unappreciative, but I really need to get back to business."

"I understand. And we appreciate the time you took to take us on a tour." Johanna said.

"It was fabulous and fascinating!" Moxie said with great enthusiasm.

"Enjoy your lunch you two, and don't make yourselves strangers. Do come back frequently.

Moxie and Johanna walked toward the restaurant. "Gee, if it hadn't been for the flower-lined walkway, I would not have known this second house is all part of the same business. When we were taking the tour, I was wondering when we'd get to the Garden Café you and Heather spoke of. I didn't realize it was in a separate structure next door. Which came first the café or the floral business?"

"Evidently, at one time the whole enterprise was in the floral business building but as that grew and this house became vacant the previous business owners scooped it up. That's when they began to struggle with too much too soon. But, now with the new owner and the professional advice they have sought, things have vastly improved, and the future looks rosy.

"Welcome Ladies! I assume you probably wish to sit outdoors on this sunny warm day?" Moxie noticed the waitress wore the same green sturdy apron as those in the flower shop, but her apron said, *"The Way to the Heart Is through the Taste Buds!"*

"Yes, and yes!" both women responded immediately.

"How's this table? Does it suit you?"

Moxie and Johanna looked at one another and smiled, Johanna spoke for both, "Just fine!"

"I like that we are nestled right in the flower bed and can see the pretty posies all around us!"

"Um-hm," agreed Johanna.

The waitress handed them two menus.

Moxie scanned the menu. "How could we go wrong with any of the choices. They look great!"

"They are. I've tried them all."

"Johanna you've spent a lot of time in this town, haven't you?"

"Yes, I'm quite involved in NNN and believe in their mission."

The NNN almost seemed like an elite club, but

Moxie had witnessed their inclusiveness at their most recent monthly meeting, and immediately knew she wanted to be a part of it.

"As I've said before, there is something very special about this little village. You can't quite explain it. It needs to be experienced. I come into town from my two-bit farm frequently on business and pleasure."

"I know there is a lot I haven't seen, but I think I've gotten a taste of the feeling already. And I happen to like it!"

"We thought you would."

There she goes again, Moxie thought. *Who was this "We" she keeps mentioning?*

"Are we ready to order ladies?" Both shook their heads yes.

"I'll have the Chimichurri Chicken Salad, please," said Moxie. She had no clue what that was, but she wanted to take a stab at saying it. Since the waitress didn't correct her, Moxie assumed she said it correctly.

"And I'll order the Lemon Herb Mediterranean Salad, please," said Johanna.

"Thanks for your orders, ladies, both salads come with a small baguette."

Moxie had no clue what was in Johanna's salad either, but she decided she'd take her old whip-smart woman friend's advice. "Moxie, let me tell ya somethin' dear heart. If you don't know what you are doing, just fudge it!" Mildred rolled her eyes every time Eunice said it.

Moxie would have loved to have wolfed the food down quickly so they could get moving and see the rest of the village, but the salad and bread was much too good not to slowly savor every morsel. The fresh herbs from the garden accentuated and complimented all the flavors. She was also enjoying the sideshow of an artist who had set up an easel in the garden. It was fun to see the white canvas filling with botanical beauty.

Toward the end of the meal Moxie excused herself and went to the Ladies Room. When she returned, Johanna stood. "Ready to head out? We have already been taken care of."

Moxie nodded. Before departing they thanked and complimented the artist and Johanna dropped a few dollars into the open lid of his hinged wooden paint box.

"Ok, we have a decision to make. Walk or drive?" They looked at one another and jointly decided some exercise wouldn't hurt, not after the meal they'd just eaten.

Chapter 9

JOHANNA AND MOXIE began walking at a good pace toward the middle of town. “Would you please slow down, woman? Don’t rush me now. I want to see every bit of this charming place.”

“Moxie! Who raised you? I can’t believe you’d speak to your elder like that!” They both laughed. It was not Moxie’s modus operandi or MO to speak so forcefully to her elders about her wants and needs. Moxie wondered where her new boldness was coming from. In Johanna’s presence she felt so comfortable it was if she was discovering more about herself and the value of friendship on a new kind of level. What a good thing.

It didn’t matter one iota, as Mildred always said, that Johanna was older than Moxie. She was a spring chicken compared to the other two Moxie found companionship with. Every time Moxie asked Eunice her age, she replied “It’s not nice to ask a very fine lady, someone like me, her age. Who the hell cares how old I am. I'm proud of the age I have reached. Not everyone gets that privilege. I wear my age like a badge of courage for all the crap I have been through!"

Mildred hated it when Eunice swore. She always clucked her tongue and said, "Eunice, would you kindly spout off more carefully? Please use more lady-like language. Thank you, my lovely."

One by one, Johanna and Moxie stopped by each business on Main Street at Moxie's pace. Since she'd never been in any of the storefronts before, they sauntered and browsed from the far end of the main drag on one side of the road then turned around and came back down the other side, toward where Johanna's car was parked at the garden shop. Every shop-owner greeted Johanna by name, and they seemed to have a great comradery between them. The positive vibes were contagious.

Each store had a sticker bearing the NNN label on it in the window and at their register. The time passed much too quickly.

When they got to the last business in the historic commercial district, Johanna turned to Moxie. "I think we've earned ourselves an ice cream cone! My treat. What do you think?"

"I'm all for it."

"Here's just the spot!" said Johanna.

"Oh, how convenient!"

The two women entered through the open door of the old-fashioned ice cream parlor. The black and white tile floor, stools that swiveled and the red leather booths made Moxie feel as if she wanted a root beer float or a gooey banana split. But Moxie quickly discovered the flavors and selections weren't old-fashioned but creative combinations. Both she and Johanna chose different "sorbets of the day" – Lemon Basil and Strawberry-Rose Geranium. They took their ices outside to the wrap-around porch, grabbed a table and dug in immediately, as if they hadn't eaten the filling lunches at the Garden Café.

"Moxie, I have a question for you – look up. Moxie looked up and read the sign on the ice cream shop which begged the question What's the Scoop?

"The scoop is that the lemon and basil combination is so refreshing just like this day has been. Highly recommended. The herb is not overpowering yet one can detect it. I feel as if I have stepped into a picture-perfect place. I loved everything I saw! The wares in the stores were unique and so beautifully presented, the shopkeepers delightful."

"Moxie, I don't want to burst your bubble, but you do know there is no such thing as perfect, right?"

"Johanna, you sure don't have to tell me that. People and places everywhere have troubles, even if it might not seem like it."

"Exactly. Hey, did you notice the trails of the garden shop all throughout town?" Moxie had a mouthful of ice-cream, so she nodded in agreement.

"Right down to the herbs in this homemade sorbet!"

"Yes, I loved the handmade soaps with rose petals in them in the bath and body shop called Soaked in Nature. And how about the aromas of the bath salts and fizz bombs. The eucalyptus-spearmint, pure bliss!" Moxie again wished she had her purse and money that Johanna insisted she leave behind. But she'd be back on a permanent basis.

"I could have spent forever in that shop. I tested nearly every aroma. I'm a walking advertisement for their store. Moxie put her wrist and then the backs of each hand up to her nose and inhaled. "Whew."

"I'm not sure you're supposed to try them all at once. You did take a bit too long in that store."

"Sorry. I could tell you were anxious to get to

the Worldly Kitchen, Johanna. That's one heck of a kitchen shop."

"Did you notice their extensive line of herbs and spices? By now you've probably figured out where some of them have been processed, too."

"Yes."

"Some of the spices not processed locally are rarely used in this part of the world so we thought having cooking classes to teach how to pair them with different foods would go over well. The lessons have been sell-outs."

When the two women finished their sorbets, they began walking back to the car. This time it was Johanna's turn to tell Moxie to slow down.

"I can't even begin to explain the energy I am feeling. It's as if the shop owners 'joie de vivre' has rubbed off on me! I feel renewed, refreshed." The only reason Moxie even knew the French term was from Mildred. She said she learned the lingo from her travels abroad one year when she was younger; back when she was "footloose and fancy free."

"That's exactly the experience we hope to achieve for our visitors here."

"Johanna, I can't thank you enough. It has been another delightful day."

"Moxie, we aren't done yet. Some of the businesses we breezed through we will return to on Easter weekend. We thought that would be a fitting time."

Moxie calculated in her head how many weeks she had left to get packed up and was happy to learn the number was dwindling.

"Johanna, I have one request. Can we put the convertible-top down on the Mini-Cooper?"

"You, betcha! You better believe it! Anything for you, my friend," said Johanna, as she slipped her jaunty hat back on that she had taken off.

Chapter 10

One day Matt called out of the blue. "Moxie, the rezoning is complete. I am free to begin showing you properties in the expanded district."

"Yay!!! Great news, Matt. I can't wait to start looking at all the potential properties."

"We've had another development. A very favorable one at that. Too much to tell you on the phone. Meet on Thursday morning at 10 a.m. at my office?"

"Sounds like a plan. Should I bring Johanna with me?"

"Not yet, Moxie."

"Ok, if you say so. See you on Thursday morning."

She could feel excitement brewing and couldn't wait to see the properties and hear more about what could be "a favorable development." Matt seemed to be a master at leaving her temporarily hanging. But her faith in Him was growing which helped keep her worries at bay.

At 10 a.m. Thursday, Matt met Moxie at the door to the real estate office. "Don't sit and get comfortable, we are headed right out to look at a property. Let's go!" Matt seemed as anxious to show the property as Moxie was to see it.

"Yes, sir! I am at your command!" Moxie wouldn't have made such as statement if they hadn't grown to be so comfortable with one another. Their friendship was deepening.

Since the real estate building was already in the commercial district they didn't have far to go. The two walked north on Main Street, took a quick right onto Middle which led to the block behind into the newly expanded commercial district and they took another right onto Union. All the while, Moxie struggled to keep up with long-legged Matt.

Matt suddenly stopped at the corner of Middle and Union, #48. Moxie looked up at the formidable two-story stone house which had a wing off to the left side with a separate entrance. The etched cornerstone notated 1780. *Wow,* Moxie thought, *that's old.* The structure reminded her of a grand old lady, timeworn, slightly haughty but her bones appeared sturdy, and nothing seemed to be sagging. Flecks in the salt and pepper granite stone sparkled.

"Oh, is this it?" asked Moxie.

"It is!"

Moxie looked at the front of the building, then stepped to the far side of the paved sidewalk, to the curb and took in the full front view. Then she went to the corner intersection of both streets taking in the perpendicular view. Some of the grand lady's silhouette was hidden by mature trees that looked as if they were planted when the ancestral house was built. An overgrowth of vines surrounded some of the windows. Lastly, Moxie walked over to the small wing which had a covered porch, the roof held up by two lathe-turned balustrades. Moxie peered into the leaded windows straddling each side of the door.

"It certainly isn't lacking in curb appeal. Someone has taken good care of this place. The vines and bushes need some trimming." Moxie suddenly regretted doing away with all of Eunice's and Mildred's antiques and collectibles. From the outside, the building looked as if it would make a stunning antiquarian shop. *Past history*, Moxie thought.

"Moxie, what are you doing looking in the window?" Matt held up the keys to the property and jangled them in front of her face. "Remember, I have the keys to the kingdom."

Moxie had to chuckle. She and Matt had been looking through windows of vacant buildings in the new part of the commercial district for so long she'd forgotten one day she'd be allowed to enter.

"I don't know Matt, this property is ...." Matt hushed her before she could get her sentence out. *Maybe*, she thought, *the apartment will be more in keeping with what I had in mind.*

"Moxie, before we enter, I have a big favor to ask of you."

"Ok. What is it?"

"Just scratch it. Erase all preconceived notions of what you are looking for. Go in with open heart and mind."

"Fair enough. I haven't even been inside yet and I'm raising objections or putting up obstacles where perhaps there are none."

"Precisely. Shall we?" He unlocked the door opening it widely, nodding for Moxie to lead the way. As they entered, she turned to Matt.

"Am I allowed to ask one question first? Then I promise you I will not ask another until I have seen the whole property."

"Ok. Fire away. One question. That's it!"

"Have you been inside before bringing me here?"

"Yes, I have."

Matt led them on a full tour inside, not rushing, taking their time going from room to room. Moxie kept her promise, she didn't ask any questions, raise objections, make any comments. Nothing. She was too busy taking in each lovely detail and the furnishings. When they were finished inside the main structure, Matt led her to the outside entrance of the wing with a two-bedroom unfurnished apartment.

Once back outside they proceeded to walk the plot of the property, finding each of the back yard boundary markers. The house and yard deceived. It was even larger than what Moxie expected.

"Now for the piece de resistance," Matt said, leading them through a narrow break in the overgrown, wild hedgerow to additional lawn bordering the river. Moxie looked at the very private hidden oasis, not saying a single word about what she was thinking.

"The back yard is half an acre which makes up for little to no front yard. Hard to find property like this in the middle of town," Matt explained. The two turned around and went back to the sidewalk in front of #48 Union. As she walked, Moxie looked down deep in thought.

"Moxie, I am surprised at your resolve! You did as I asked. Now I have another request. Go home, jot down all your questions and sleep on what you saw. Make a list of the positives and negatives and your questions. Note what you liked and what you didn't."

"Oh, Matt! You have got to be kidding. What do you think I am? How do I put this without being politically incorrect? Well, do you think I am a deaf-mute? How do you think I can look at a property like this without wanting to ask immediate questions...I mean..."

Contrary to his nature, Matt hushed her and didn't seem to want to hear anything Moxie had to say.

She felt her chest tightening. "Matt, look, don't shush me! I am not an unopinionated simpleton! I have questions, comments and concerns galore. I am even baffled as to why you'd even show me this property!"

"I'm sure you do have plenty to say, and I will answer all of your questions and concerns." He looked at his watch. "But not today. I have another appointment, and time has gotten away. I need to run."

Before Moxie could reply, Matt took off like a greyhound out at the racetrack. Then he turned, and yelled out, "I'll call you in the morning and we will set a time to get together. I promise. Write down all you are thinking." Moxie watched him getting smaller as he made his way down the sidewalk and finally when she could see him no more, she walked back to her car stammering.

After dinner, Moxie received a text message. *Meet me at the office at 10 a.m. tomorrow ~ Matt*. Moxie wasn't thrilled to have to wait until ten in the morning. She liked early starts but what could she do?

Chapter 11

MATT WAS WAITING FOR HER at the front door of the real estate office when she arrived on Thursday. He took Moxie upstairs to his office and closed the door.

"Matt, I gotta say it before I burst at the seams. Thanks for a whole lotta nothing! What were you thinking showing me that property at #48 Union?"

"Hold on Moxie! Be patient, I have an explanation. Let me get down to it."

Moxie was so stirred up she didn't even notice Johanna sitting there. When she finally saw her, Moxie made no attempt at cordial greetings. Matt took the chair from the corner and moved it into the seating area for Moxie.

"One question. Johanna, have you seen the property Matt showed me the other day at #48 Union?"

"Yes, Moxie, I have." Moxie felt as if she had steam coming out her ears. And then she began to feel bad. What business did she have lighting into Matt like that? Guilt began to needle. She felt snarky and was afraid to open her mouth and say more. Afraid what might come out that she'd regret later. *Hold on, give them a chance Moxie,* she said to herself.

"Moxie, do you remember I said there has been an unexpected development?"

"Yes."

"Well, a few days ago, I received a call. I need to honor the caller's anonymity. Anyway, he seems to see all. I'm sure he's been watching what's going on with the commercial expansion as well as with the Neighbor-to-Neighbor Network. If you'll listen, he has an interesting proposition for you and me."

"For you and me?" Moxie leaned back, then forward at attention.

"Hear me out, Moxie. Eunice and Mildred had his assistance for decades. He's aware of, and impressed with, how you have taken a life of nothing and made something of yourself. He said he thinks you are just getting started and sees enormous potential."

"In me? Well, I can't take full credit for that. Mildred and Eunice played an enormous part in my development. They were wonderful mentors."

Johanna spoke up. "Moxie don't minimize this. You're deserving of all he thinks about you."

"Thank you. I appreciate your vote of confidence too. I really do."

"So, about the property we looked at yesterday. You must have so many questions and I can't even imagine what you are thinking. I shouldn't have run off on you yesterday, but I had to. My appointment was important to you, to me. All four of us collectively."

"What four? You, me and the guy you have been conniving with? And who else?"

Matt looked over at Johanna. "And me. Moxie don't be so suspicious. There are good intentions behind it."

"Matt, I'm sorry, it's just that you have left me hanging two times now. Perhaps I am feeling a little distrustful. I don't understand what you've got in your mind. Frankly, I think you've lost your marbles! What were you doing showing me a property that is perfectly suited to a bed and breakfast or something like that? I mean...twelve bedrooms, twelve private baths, a huge state of art commercial kitchen, common spaces large enough for meetings, group dining, socializing or what not.

And then the little wing to the side where a person like me could live more than comfortably. But never once did you indicate that space was what you had in mind for me. And then the incredible outdoors acreage behind the building. I mean, it's like Eden back there. And it's nearly turnkey. But the rents...I can't even imagine what kind of a mortgage I'd need. How much dough do you think I was left with? Whatever you think, you are completely off base, Matt! The place is tremendous."

"Twelve bedrooms and twelve bathrooms? Come on Moxie, don't you think you are exaggerating a little bit?"

"Well, yeah, maybe...but Matt."

"Hold on, hold on, calm down, Moxie. I have question for you."

Moxie decided she'd better keep quiet. She was getting herself all stirred up again.

"What would it mean to have a real fresh start?"

"I will, as soon as I can find a new place to live and move myself there."

"That's not what I mean. Here's the thing – the big guy wants to recruit you to help carry out his vision. He wants to take the property I showed you and turn it into an example and eventually take the model elsewhere. What he has in mind could very well become a shining example for other small towns."

"What I am trying to say is we've been offered a good opportunity. Moxie, please listen to Johanna."

"Moxie, I think you and Matt have what it will take. You overhauled a worn-out business, with no previous experience in management and that was quite admirable."

"That's what I'm trying to tell you, Moxie. You had what it took to put a business back on a firm foundation again. You have experience and talent that even you didn't know you had. That's why the investor believes in you for this new venture. He says you have so much to give."

"Wait a minute, wait a minute. Johanna, you know exactly what I've been left with and you also know most of it will be used as legacy funds and how they must be used to continue what Eunice and Mildred started."

"I'm getting to that." Johanna stood, and asked Moxie and Matt to do the same and to move close to her and each other. Now, let's take a breather for three minutes and we will start again. They stood silently looking down. To Moxie the time seemed interminable.

"Moxie, give me your hand. Matt, give me your hand." Both extended their hands and she proceeded to put Moxie's hand into Matt's.

"Moxie, meet Matt. Matt, meet Moxie." They

shook hands. "After spending time with both of you individually and knowing what you need to do with your individual legacy funds, you've been charged with directing, you two are the perfect match for each other in this venture. Helping others and using one's creativity is important to both of you, is it not?"

They both nodded their heads to the affirmative. Lowering her voice to a whisper, Johanna turned to Matt, "You've demonstrated how successful you are in real estate, but your wish is to get back into the kitchen and use your creative talents. Correct?"

"Correct!" Matt said loudly and firmly. "You don't have to whisper Johanna, it's ok. I've been very upfront. This place knows my plan, and they're good with it."

"Moxie, well...you are a living testimony of someone who found a whole new life in the fiber arts and by unleashing God given skills you didn't even know you possessed. Your story is compelling."

"What the investor sees in you both are two people who can be at the foundation of a new enterprise to give women a chance at making a solid living in creative ways if given new beginnings with starter funds, mentoring, education and the right opportunities."

Broad smiles came across the faces of both Moxie and Matt when they realized where Johanna was going. "Moxie, this would fulfill your obligation to give back using the legacy funds Mildred and Eunice have left. Matt, you've mentioned to me so many times how several of your very successful sisters helped you to become the wonderful man you have become. What do you say? Join forces in this opportunity, and I will be right in it, too. It will be a place where all kinds of art, creativity and faith can thrive under one roof and make a real difference to women."

Matt exhaled loudly, as if he'd been holding his breath all morning and was finally relieved of the pressure.

"Matt, I bet you've got some sisters who would definitely be on board with the concept." Matt nodded and Johanna smiled.

"It sounds like this will meet the requirements." Moxie had read the letters left behind for her by Mildred and Eunice so many times, she'd memorized their requests by heart, word for word.

What we want most for you is health and happiness and everything else will fall into place. No reason for worry. That having been said, it is important for us to leave a legacy and to continue to give back. There is a stipulation. Paying it forward must be for a cause that makes your heart zing, too. Our preference is to continue to support young women and their business pursuits. Sixty percent of each of our estates, must be used for this purpose. I've assigned Attorney Loyal Thomas to manage and oversee this and we've hired Johanna Harrison as a non-profit business consultant.

Moxie sat quietly considering working with Matt once again. She reminded herself how she always liked working with him even though it was only at a donut shop. He was such a decent guy-- it was no wonder so many locals were loyal to the pastry grease pit. Nothing-special food yet the customers came for the camaraderie – Matt's hospitality, good nature and his community involvement was held in high regard by Mildred and Eunice. "It's the next best place to get a bite besides the Open Doors Soup and Sandwich Shop," the two women always touted, and of course Matt knew how Eunice felt about the chocolate donuts.

"Moxie, I'm pleased your store manager has offered to buy you out of the sewing shop. The investor needs you and Matt to drive what he has in mind without any encumbrances. The offer has been well thought out. It will provide you with everything you need so your only concern will be the tasks you will been given. It will be an exciting venture. He is willing to fully commit to you if you will commit to Him and to me."

Moxie said nothing. She and Matt sat quietly. She was thinking about the huge investment and risk they'd be taking. Or would they? The community already had so much going for it. It was why Moxie was willing to take her own chances to move there.

"So, tell me, what do we need to do other than work our butts off?" Matt looked at Moxie and smiled.

"Work with me to rally the troops and build on something with great promise and opportunity! Our task will be to collaborate and carry out the vision. What this fella has in mind will be at the heart and soul of NNN. It will become an even more special community than it is already. Caring people all working toward something good and exciting all together is always a recipe for success, don't you think Matt?"

"Absolutely."

"Matt, do think you could work with me again? I mean, you did have to fire me."

"Oh, come on, Moxie, don't be silly. We were both at completely different stages and places in our lives back then. I'm willing to put faith in you, and I hope you'll do the same for me.

Let's leave the past behind and move forward together. Can we?"

"Yes!" Moxie said, feeling the blessed assurance she needed.

"There is one other important stipulation. The one who has called us will want The Community Church to be included in some way in the overall plan. They will have their own role and we will learn more about that in coming days if you'll agree to it."

"I think we need to begin meeting more frequently, don't you?" asked Matt.

"Yes," said Johanna.

The thought of seeing more of their sage business consultant Johanna and Matt was a happy thought that made Moxie's stomach squirmy.

"I've given you enough to think about. Decision #1 – Are you in or out? Decision #2 – Will #48 Union be the right space for us? To decide that, Moxie and Matt, we will need to delve into more specifics of a women's creative wellness center we've vaguely been dreaming of. No pressure except I would like to say, the other investor has made a difference in my life. It's what has led me to this place and the community work I do."

It's all for you, Lord, it's, all for you, Johanna

thought as she sat and listened to Moxie and Matt talk back and forth a little more about what they'd just discussed.

Chapter 12

MOXIE AWOKE WITH A JOLT. She could feel a pulsing of energy going through her body in every fiber of her being. Where has this sensation come from? All she knew is she needed to get rid of it; do something with the pent-up tension before it did something unfortunate with her.

The sewing store hadn't opened yet, so she called Beverly, her manager, on her cell phone. "Beverly, it's Moxie. How are you?" Moxie didn't wait for her answer. "Who is on the schedule with you today?"

Moxie was silent as Beverly told her. "Listen. Do you think the three of you can handle the store today? I have some errands I need to run, and I may be gone for a while. Tuesdays are typically a little slower, so I thought this would be a good day for me to tend to some things."

"Don't you worry, we will be fine. Remember,

we are going to have to get used to not having you around here anymore. Is everything ok, Moxie?"

"No worries! Except I have ants in my pants," Moxie refrained from saying more.

She made herself a quick cup of coffee and a couple pieces of toast which she ate and drank while she showered and dressed. Moxie looked in her closet for something to wear. She shoved clothes hanger after clothes hanger aside. Rejecting everything in front of her. None of the clothes in her closet seemed to reflect the way she was feeling. *I have got to do something about this wardrobe*, thought Moxie. *Everything hanging in the closet looked like it was made for Miss Prudy of yesteryear*. She had never thought of her wardrobe that way before. For lack of anything to wear that really inspired her or seemed a little unconventional.

Moxie finally settled once again on her favorite pair of jeans, her one and only boho top and she slipped on her favorite perky orange flats. At least they had a little zip to them. Knowing it was the best she could do, she shrugged her shoulders at her reflection in her full-length mirror, grabbed her purse and out the door she went.

She knew not where she was going in the new car she was driving. Weeks prior she'd taken Mildred's large vintage blue Buick four-door sedan and traded it in for what Mildred would have referred to as a little "June bug." An orange energy efficient hybrid she was quite satisfied with. What a day that was when Moxie signed the papers for her first car, and to top it off it was brand new.

Before she knew it, she was at her destination. "Little June Bug," she said aloud to the vehicle that led her there, "thank you for bringing me back to 'Belle Aire.'" Moxie got out of the car, turned in a circle and marveled once again at the beauty of The Way to the Heart Is Through the Garden, where she parked.

As soon as she walked into the garden shop, she was greeted by two women she'd met previously, Heather and Helena. She was warmed by the fact they remembered her name.

"So, what brings you in today?" asked Helena.

"I came in to browse and to purchase a few things I'd seen when I was here last without my purse."

"Would you like us to just leave you to your vices?" asked Heather.

"Let's go get what I want, then I will browse to see if anything else. Can you hold my purchases at the register while I walk through town? I am concerned about leaving plants in the hot car if I get hung up shop hoping."

"Sounds good. Now, what was it you want?"

asked Heather. Moxie had decided even though she had no idea where she'd be living, she was going to take a leap of faith and hope she'd find a good place to use what she was purchasing.

"One of those fabulous dried gourd birdhouses and a small aralia plant which I saw back in the exotic plant section last time I was here."

First, they went to the bird section and got the dried gourd birdhouse. She really liked the earthy color of the one she'd chosen. Then she and Heather went back to the greenhouse where the aralias were. "You know what, I think I will get two aralias, a small one for me and then a larger one for my friend, Johanna." Moxie read the tag in the plant. "Yes, I think Johanna will like this plant, and I'll pick out a beautiful pot so I can take it out of the plastic one." The two women then proceeded to the pot section and together they figured out the correct size and a beautiful pot to compliment the plant. It's the least she could do to thank Johanna for the kindness she had shown since the loss of Mildred and Eunice.

"You know, Heather, I think that will be all for today. I have many other shops to hit. I'll save my browsing for another day. It will give me an excuse to come back, and I may even need to start a second terrarium in the future." Moxie paid for her purchases and Heather put them in a box down under the counter with Moxie's name on them.

"I'll be back in a few hours to get my purchases." Moxie said when she left and proceeded up town.

Moxie didn't think she could have enjoyed her trip through Main Street any more than the first time, but she found as she went from shop to shop her senses were even more acutely tuned in this time. She listened to what she was hearing in the shops and watched interactions of people. Delightful mood music played in every shop. The happy banter between store clerks indicated a wonderful camaraderie. Perhaps the NNN had something to do with it.

Moxie observed one shopkeeper bringing the newspaper in off the stoop for the neighboring store, another swept his stoop and then proceeded down the line sweeping others. One of the shopkeepers was watering all the window boxes up and down the street.

When Moxie was in Parchment Papers, the stationery shop picking out a handmade card to accompany the gift for Johanna the owner of the deli came to say good morning and to announce the day's specials and take orders from the store clerks. Every greeting card in the stationery shop was one-of-a-kind created by local photographers, water colorists and graphic artists. They had the largest selection of unique pop up cards and origami cards Moxie had ever seen. Moxie could have spent an entire day looking. Who would have known this little village had so much of interest? Moxie saw gestures of kindness everywhere.

The kitchen shop had what Moxie would call a “test kitchen” and they were cranking warm cinnamon candied pecans out of the ovens and brewing up coffee samples. While Moxie was in the The Worldly Kitchen she heard the owner tell his employees he’d be back soon. He was going to take coffee and paper cones full of pecans down to the travel agent on the corner, the hair salon owner and to the Reverend at the Community Church, the lone church in town. “Today, it’s their turn,” he said, as if every morning he routinely made deliveries to his fellow citizens.

She made a few purchases as she went through town to add to the gift box she was planning for Johanna. A beautiful linen kitchen towel with botanical graphics from the kitchen shop coordinated beautifully with the pot for the new plant she purchased. She’d also include a marjoram infused balsamic vinegar, a few flower shaped soaps from the bath and body shop Soaked in Nature with a handcrafted ceramic soap dish made by a local artisan. She couldn’t pass up two sachets filled with lavender, one for herself and one for Johanna. She was so pleased with all she purchased.

As Moxie had nearly completed her round, she noticed there was a hair salon next to What's the Scoop? She listened to sounds of friendly chatter coming out of the shop. "*Halo! Come In, Welcome to Angel Locks*" said the blackboard which propped open the door. Then, just as her "Little June Bug" had led her to town earlier that morning, something led Moxie fully inside the door. A woman came over to greet her. "Hi! I am Angela, I hold the key. I'm the owner. How can we help you today?"

"Gee, I didn't know I was coming in till just this moment. I'm not quite sure why I am here. Although, I suppose I do need a haircut."

"You're here, why not?" Angela asked.

"You're right. It's a good day for a haircut."

"Come on over to my chair. What's your name?"

"Moxie!" Angela put a cream-colored cape that felt like gossamer around Moxie's neck and spread the fabric over her lap.

"Hey, I like your name! How about we give you a cut that's more fitting? Looks like you've had the same style for a long time."

"Whoa, slow down! I'm not sure I am ready for drastic change!"

"Nah, change is good. You'll see. Put faith in me!"

Moxie swallowed hard as she remembered Johanna's words "GO BOLD" a few months back.

"Ok, Angela, total transformation! My faith is in you, don't mess up!"

Moxie watched Angela look to the sky as she reached for her scissors. "Wait a minute Moxie, give me a few minutes. I need to get a vision!"

Heaven help me, Moxie thought.

"Ok, ok, it's coming to me now. You know what I am going to do? An asymmetric style. And since we are starting with long hair. I've got plenty to play with."

In her nervousness, Moxie scratched her head. "What does that mean anyway? Asymmetric style?"

"You'll see!"

"I guess I will. Cut away. I have full faith in you. I think I'll just close my eyes, relax and give into the experience."

"That's a girl, you do that." Moxie closed her eyes and never once opened them until the stylist was done with the total makeover. In truth, Moxie didn't have the guts to. She was shaking in her orange pumps. Her cut hadn't changed much since she was a kid.

"Moxie is this your natural hair color?"

"Gosh, Angela, I can hardly remember. For a while there I was goth and every color of the Kool Aid palette. But yeah, it's pretty much back to basic mousey brown now."

"Well, I am gonna give you some golden honey highlights so when people look at your head, they'll say Well!! Halo fabulous!"

Angela seemed to be the queen of bad puns and swift scissors. Moxie had given her free reign, so she didn't argue.

When her hair styling was done, Angela asked Moxie if she wanted a manicure and painted nails. By then Moxie had deeply given into the experience and still wasn't ready to open her eyes.

"Sure, why not?" she said dreamily.

As Angela worked on her nails Moxie tried to stay in the zone of meditating and ruminating on what she'd seen and experienced while walking through each store.

Angela put Moxie to ease. The occasional words that were passed between them were meaningful. They discussed how a tweak to one's appearance can bring metamorphosis. Their conversation was never small talk or gossip driven, which always made Moxie uncomfortable in hair salons. By the time Angela had finished working her magic, Moxie had made a big decision. *This! This!* Moxie thought, *is what I need more of – self-care.*

When Angela was finished Moxie opened her eyes and looked at herself in the mirror. She could barely believe what she was seeing. She blinked and put her hand up to her head feeling the short length of her hair. It felt strange. She'd never had such cropped hair before. The highlights accentuated a brilliance in her eyes she'd never previously noticed. Moxie liked what she saw. She liked it very much.

"Oh, Angela! Wow! You are a wizard with the scissors. I feel like a different person. Is it really me I'm seeing in the mirror?"

"It's you, Moxie, all you. You were hidden behind all that hair, and now your countenance can be seen, and you are beautiful."

Moxie looked down at the shiny bright red enamel on her fingernails. She wasn't quite so sure about that. She considered herself a "less-is-more kind of girl" and having coated nails seemed a little over top and a little too far from a more natural look. Covering up her nails, part of her overall countenance that had just been uncovered, seemed somehow out of sync. *Ah, well*, Moxie thought, *at least I've gone bold for the day*. The polish could be removed easily but the hair! The style was there to stay. It made her feel fresh and a little bit cheeky. Like what she was looking for in her closet earlier that morning, but she couldn't find it anywhere other than in her bright orange pumps that matched her car.

Moxie poured out well-deserved compliments on Angela, paid the bill, tipping her generously. She walked out of the shop feeling like the girl in the show Mildred and Eunice watched on the throwback channel on TV, "That Girl."

Moxie began walking to her car, and suddenly turned circle deciding to backtrack to a few of the boutique clothing stores. With her new do, the clothing she was wearing seemed more out of date and she thought it was time to begin doing something about it right here, right now.

"May I help you?" the saleswoman asked.

"Yes, please do!" Moxie allowed herself to be open to the saleswoman's good suggestions. After purchasing her third outfit, one from Artful Threads and two at All Dun Up, she decided it was time to go. She had a good start to an updated wardrobe. Any other purchases would come slowly and very thoughtfully. After all, Eunice had put a lot of effort into teaching Moxie not to be a spendthrift. It's how they kept the sewing shop in good financial health.

Moxie asked the salesperson in All Dun Up, the last clothing store she visited if she could wear the clothing home once paid for.

"Do you want me to discard your old jeans and top?"

Just as she was ready to say yes, she had a change of heart. Before getting her new clothing, the boho top was her most updated shirt and getting rid of her favorite jeans would be like dumping an old but loyal friend. "No, on second thought if you'll put the old clothes in a bag, I'll take them with me. One man's trash is another man's treasure. I'll donate them to a good cause," she said, hoping the woman didn't think she was completely loopy.

Silly as it was, Moxie walked out of the store laughing when the sales lady broke out into song, "I'm all 'dun up,' ready for the ride, now I've hit my stride."

Moxie picked up the pace and walked back to her car. Before heading out, she needed to pick up her purchases at the counter of the garden shop. Moxie went through the open door and was met by Heather.

Heather said welcome to Moxie as if she was a new customer and hadn't seen her a few hours previously. Suddenly, Heather made a realization. She put two fingers in her mouth and let out a piercing whistle. "Well! Look at you, Moxie! I'm nearly speechless! Ooh-la-la! You found Angela down at Angel's Locks, didn't you? Or maybe she found you. Holy Wow! She worked her legendary magic."

Moxie turned in a circle with a huge grin on her face. "So, you like it, huh? So do I. Makes me wonder why I didn't change things up sooner."

"You probably just weren't quite ready." Heather and Moxie visited for a few more minutes talking about her new "asymmetrical style."

"Look, I've got to run, I've spent much more time here intown today than I planned. I've gotten an entire makeover that I didn't know was going to be part of my plan for today. But I'll be back soon. I have some work to do to transform my life even further and I want to brainstorm with you."

Heather helped Moxie carry her purchases out to the car noticing Heather had already transplanted the larger of the two plants, the one she planned to give to Johanna into the new pot. She was grateful for her kindness.

The two women said their goodbyes and Moxie drove on, anxious to reach Sew the Heart before closing. She couldn't wait to surprise the girls with the start of what was only the beginning of a lifestyle transformation.

However, Moxie got railroaded by "Little June Bug." She had plans of her own.

Chapter 13

BEFORE SHE KNEW IT, she and "Little Miss June Bug" were sitting in front of a pub near the border of where the old district and expanded new commercial district on Union Street met. Moxie sat in the car and listened to her stomach growl. The only thing she'd eaten all day were two pieces of buttered toast and coffee. She looked at the clock on her cell and it was 5 p.m. Already! How had that happened? It wasn't a waste of a day, that's for sure.

John Peter's Pub was right in front of her. *Why not?* Moxie thought, *another new experience to add to the list today. Taking myself out to dinner at a "real" restaurant, not fast food.*

Moxie walked into the dark paneled, smokey pub which was not at all what she hoped to find. The place reminded her of a rathskeller she went into one night with her troublemaker foster brother years ago. A night she tried hard to forget.

"Good evening. Sit wherever you want. I will be right with you, with a menu. Moxie looked around and noticed the other early bird diners. She chose a table for two over against the far wall and the waitress arrived as soon as she sat down.

"Do you have any San Pellegrino?"

"Yes, straight up or blood orange flavored? Which do you prefer?"

"I'll take the flavored, thanks."

"Be right back to get your order." Moxie opened the menu and read the line at the top.

One cannot think well, love well,
sleep well, if one has not dined well.
-Virginia Woolf

She scanned the menu and decided she didn't want a full dinner even though she ought to. She'd spent enough time out. Feeling weary she wanted to eat quickly and get home. The items on Bar Room Bites part of the menu looked enticing. She settled on a small plate of poutine and a house salad. She wasn't quite sure what poutine was but the description of fries, local Belle Aire cheese curds and hot gravy struck just right as being what she wanted to fill the empty spot in her tummy.

The tables in the pub began to fill as she ate. She'd made a great choice and finished every last fry on the plate and all of the salad, which was quite a step up from the iceberg lettuce at the place she frequented with Mildred. She was just getting ready to leave when she heard familiar voices. One sounded like Matt. She left enough cash for the bill and a tip, stood up and walked toward the door.

"Moxie, is that you?" She turned in the direction of the voice.

"Well, I'll be darned, Matt, it is her. You are right!" Moxie looked at Johanna.

"Johanna and I saw you when we came in, and we were sitting here arguing whether it was you or not. We decided if it was you, you've gone underground on Union. Your appearance has changed so drastically."

"It's the asymmetrical cut, I bet."

"Holy wow! Did you do that to yourself today, girl?" Johanna asked.

"I did! Not quite sure what got into me!" Moxie's hand with freshly painted red fingernails went up to her head. She'd completely forgotten about her new look while she ate because she was so involved in enjoying her newfound love. A plate of poutine.

There was a third person sitting with Matt and

Johanna. It was the pastor she'd met at the NNN meeting held at the Community Church.

"Nice to see you again, Moxie," said Reverend Bridges.

"Moxie! You took away all my fun!" Johanna said with her lip turned down.

"What do you mean?"

"Well, your make-over! You beat us too it. It was going to be our Easter treat to you."

Who was this "us and we" Johanna kept referring to? Moxie wondered.

"Yeah, well. I'm not quite sure what led me into the hair salon next to What's the Scoop? this afternoon.

"Angela had her way with you, didn't she?" Johanna and Matt gushed more over Moxie's new appearance.

"I tried to contact you earlier in the day to see if you could join us, and when I couldn't reach you, I decided perhaps it was best that I meet with just Matt and the pastor to discuss some aspects of our new project and how the Community Church could be helpful with that. Matt has already given me his commitment to the project. Like I said, no pressure, Moxie. I want you to be completely comfortable with whatever decision you make, whether to join us or not."

"I don't want to crash your party. But I've been

struggling. I'd love some feedback. I'm glad the pastor is here."

Matt jumped up, grabbed an empty chair from a nearby table for Moxie.

"By all means while we are all here, unburden your heart," said the pastor. All three moved their chairs closer and leaned in toward Moxie so they could talk quietly.

Just be open, Moxie said to herself. "Well, I'm not struggling with the idea of working with Matt again, and I feel good that we will get all the necessary support we need to make a non-profit venture successful. I feel confident of that. Johanna, I don't think Matt and I could ask for a better business coach."

Matt nodded in agreement.

Moxie paused and looked over at the pastor, not knowing how to best communicate her thoughts about what was a stumbling block preventing her from jumping in with the project. "I'm feeling such heavy obligation toward due diligence in making sure however I handle the funds I've been left with, would meet with Eunice and Mildred's approval. They worked so hard for all they earned, and it was not easy. I heard the stories of their personal challenges – their strife and struggle. I want to make sure the funds go to the right people and project. They are meant for good-hearted people like Eunice and Mildred, who may have had a bad stroke of luck, or have found themselves in unfortunate situations or have had unknown monsters in the closet that have reared their heads...you know."

"That's one of reasons the church has been asked to join in on this new venture we are envisioning, Moxie. We are privy to information that aids with good decision-making in that regard. And faith and creativity have been partners for a long, long time. Art and spirituality fit together naturally," said the pastor. "Think back through the ages of the magnificent art that is in churches – mosaic works, fresco paintings, carvings, sculptures not even to mention stained glass."

They sat quietly giving Moxie time to think about what was said. Finally, the pastor spoke up again. "Is there anything else that's concerning to you, Moxie?"

"Well, to be honest, I'm not sure whether Eunice and Mildred had a secular or non-secular approach to what they began so many years ago, supporting start-ups for women in business. I could never quite figure those two out sometimes. For instance, whenever the subject of faith came up there was a lot of good-natured talk about it, but I was never quite sure where they really stood on some issues. Take for example the evening before Eunice and Mildred left for their fatal joy ride. Miss Eunice looked at me and said out of the blue, 'Moxie, please don't ever take me for a heathen. I worship every time I pop a piece of chocolate in my mouth. I feel all the spiritual things one is supposed to feel when chocolate preys on my tongue – gratitude, compassion for those who are without and hope that the next chocolate blessing will not be too far off. I am still working on my generosity and sharing. Those chocolate caramel concoctions, I can horde them like no other and fudge, good grief! Don't even go there. I'm not willing to part with one blessed morsel. Not even for my dear Toby before he became deceased, a dead pup-pup.' Then Eunice continued. 'I've got a whole new list of the saints who will provide me with guidance. There's St. Lindt, St. Godiva, St. Ferrero Rocho, St. Toblerone, St. Ghirardelli. Why, I'm set for life, but, please,' she said, 'don't ever look at me as a saint, I'm still learning to repent of my sins.'"

The pastor laughed until tears ran down his checks. Moxie was not sure if he ever knew Eunice and Mildred, but the pastor appreciated the humor anyway.

"Now, help me guys! What am I supposed to make of that?" They all shook their heads.

"We will leave that up to you!" said Matt.

"God, the lady was a stitch! Sometimes, when banter like that occurred, I wondered if Eunice hadn't missed her calling – life on the big stage. Oh, how I miss her and her dear, sweet sidekick, Mildred. They brought so much light to my life in a time when there was only darkness."

"How fortunate you were to have known them so well. Eunice was given a gift when she was put on this earth. Her own unique way of communicating. Aren't we grateful she shared it with us through her good humor?" asked Reverend Bridges. All nodded their heads in agreement.

"Ok. Back to serious business," said Johanna, "Moxie, do you think it would help you if you attended a few Sunday services at the Community Church just to get a better feel for how the folks there contribute to Belle Aire and her people?"

"Yes, I'd like that."

Pastor Bridges leaned in closer to Moxie. "Can I tell you a little secret?"

Moxie nodded her head yes.

"I've known the two women of whom you speak for a long, long time. And religion is not always loud, boisterous, and in the face. Sometimes, faith works in silent actions and God's work is shown through ordinary people who help build God's community."

Moxie sat very still thinking about all Mildred and Eunice had done for women that she was never aware of until they left this earth.

"Thank you, Pastor Bridges for that tidbit. Look, I'm sorry I crashed your party of three. I've been out all day. I'm going to head home." Moxie stood from her chair and Matt pulled it aside for her, "If you want to go with me to church, meet me at the office on Sunday at 9:30. If you change your mind or would rather go alone, no problem."

"Thanks all, for listening. My heart feels much lighter."

"Same with ours. Enjoy the rest of your evening," said the pastor.

Chapter 14

EARLY SUNDAY MORNING Moxie decided to go to church. She could remember few times she'd ever gone before. She had a very vague memory of one of her foster mothers taking her and her natural-born children to church occasionally. Perhaps, that foster mother was one of the most "even" of them all. But long ago, Moxie had decided to try to forget all except one.

Matt said to call if she decided to go to church, but she was a big girl. Why did she need someone hold her hand and take her there? As she dressed in her new turquoise floral skirt with the flounce at the bottom and coordinating shirt, she kept looking at herself in the mirror. She rarely wore a skirt or dress because many of her workdays were spent in front of the sewing machine. If she went ahead with the new proposed project, life was going to take on a whole new dimension besides her town of residence. She'd have to dress decently for work.

Moxie tooted along in her "Little June Bug" feeling good about her new appearance. She parked in the church parking lot, climbed up the white marble steps and walked in through the open doors of The Community Church. A familiar looking woman came over. "Good Morning, very nice to see you again on this pretty sunny day." She handed Moxie a program and as Moxie walked down the aisle to find a seat it came to her. The woman who greeted her was Angela. The one responsible for her spiffy new haircut.

Moxie chose a pew in the middle section of the church, its size deceiving. From the exterior of the building, it looked quite large however, the main sanctuary was simple and intimate, devoid of decoration other than a few religious icons. She sat comfortably and quietly looking at the bulletin until she felt movement beside her. It was Matt. He sat so close she felt his oxford shirt rubbing her bare arms. She scooted over a little, just enough to give them both little elbow room. "I didn't think you were coming. Glad to see you're here." They smiled at one another and looked at their programs.

As people filed into the church, the noise increased with chatter, laughter, handshakes and hugs. Moxie always envisioned churches filled with reverent silence every Sunday morning, but as she sat and observed, she better understood why Mildred and Eunice probably made their faces known here. The behind-the-scenes social butterflies that they were, they loved being involved with the community which became even more clear to Moxie once they were no longer around.

Suddenly the organ struck up music, people came to their feet and reached out to the neighbor on each side of them in the pew.

Matt clasped hands with the person on his right and Moxie on his left, whispering to her, "Don't worry I am lost in the dark on this song, too."

Come, enter this place
Come, bring all races
Sing we out loud
Hear, all, the sound

Moxie relaxed as she clasped hands with Matt and the woman to her left and listened to the beautiful lyrics people knew well. No one used song books, so Moxie figured they probably sang the tune each week. When the song ended all sat down.

"Good morning, everyone! If you've never been here before, my name is Reverend Thad Bridges."

He was dressed in casual khakis pants and a collared button-down shirt.

Moxie leaned over to Matt and whispered, "What kind of church is this anyway? I never thought to ask."

"All I know is their sign out front says non-denominational – all are welcomed." Matt put his finger up to his lips as if to say "Shhhh...."

The pastor continued speaking from the altar. "I don't know about you, but I was ready to get down on my knees after some of those loud cracks of thunder last night." People in the pews laughed and nodded their heads at his remark.

Moxie's chat with Reverend Bridges at John Peter's Pub several nights previously was comforting, and many concerns she had in her mind were settled. By his response to her Eunice story, the guy had a healthy sense of humor.

"So, now we come to our time of sharing our joys and concerns."

A man rose and spoke with what sounded like an accent. "I'd just like to say Merci, Mes Amis." As you all know, I live over my shop, and I looked out the window last night during the storm and saw my trash bin had been knocked over and was rolling down the sidewalk. Trash was strewn everywhere.

As soon as the lightning and thunder stopped, I got out my galoshes, put on my Macintosh and went down to retrieve the trash bin. Some good soul had beat me too it. It had been up righted, put back in its place, and all the rubbish had been picked up and the top was securely on it. Thank you, my friend, whoever you are."

A little girl sitting in the front pew rose next. "I'm worried. I can't find my kitty. He was outside when it started raining and he hasn't come home yet." Awwwww...could be heard throughout the room. "My mommy said my kitty will be found because people around here look out for one another and for kitties and doggies, too. Please, if you see my little Oliver, will you bring him home to me?" Her mom stood, "We live at 26 Chestnut, and Oliver is sort of a caramel or chestnut-colored tabby."

The pastor bowed his head. "Dear God, please watch out for Eliza's kitty. Please protect Oliver and show him the way home. Amen." The little girl stood again. "Please tell God to tell Oliver not to bring any mice home with him. Mommy doesn't like that." The pastor bowed his head again and gave in to the little girl's prayer request.

A voice spoke out from the back of the church. Moxie turned and saw it was Helena from the garden center. "I don't mean to embarrass anyone, but I'd just like to say welcome to a visitor we have today. Perhaps she will stick around afterward and introduce herself."

The Reverend spoke up. "We extend a warm welcome to any newcomers we have today. Thank you, Helena. It's always a good Sunday when we have new faces in the crowd."

A woman sitting next to Johanna about her same age, stood up next. "Just a quick reminder. Third Thursday is coming up. You all know what that means. We're in need of a few set up and clean up people for our NNN community dinner. Any volunteers?" A whole host of hands shot up. "Tell you what, anyone who can arrive early or stay late, we can use you. So just keep that in mind and we will trust we'll have enough helping hands as usual. We always have more than enough food. Remember to mark any casserole dishes or bowls or what have you with your name, so we know who they should go home with. I acknowledge and thank the kind person who donated all the food to last month's meeting. We were in a terrible jam when the family who does a lion's share of cooking all came down with flu." Matt looked over at Moxie and quietly mouthed thank you.

The pastor stepped in to speak. "Set up will begin at 5:30 p.m. as usual, dinner served from

6 to 7:30 p.m. and stick around afterward for the NNN meeting till we kick you out. Look forward to seeing everyone on Third Thursday.

"Our theme this month is Awe and Wonder. So, I'll look forward to hearing words, a story, an image or a song from anyone who wishes to participate in our worship. All month long we welcome you to share with us what has captured your attention or your imagination or what has awoken your curiosity about this beautiful universe of ours."

Matt and Moxie sat attentively as they watched the unfolding of a service which had a cohesive, unifying message to it through the readings, music, and the pastor's words. Moxie liked Reverend Bridge's relaxed, mostly off the cuff, not over practiced, well-communicated style of delivery filled with relatable life lessons. His sermon on New Beginnings gave Moxie a lot to think about.

When the service ended, Matt and Moxie stood. People seated in front and behind them shook their hands and said good morning or have a good week or some other gesture of hospitality. Filled pews were testimony enough for Moxie that the people liked what they had going on Sunday mornings at the Community Church.

"Ahhh...," said Moxie to a man who extended

his hand, "You're the man who roasts up those candied pecans down at the kitchen shop."

"Yes, I am Kirk, the owner of The Worldly Kitchen."

"Have you sampled my pecans? Do you like them?"

"I don't know what I like better the taste or the yummy smell. How can anyone possibly walk by your shop without wanting to go in and buy what you have cookin' up!"

"We sell a boat load of them. The pecan farms down in the deep south must love us." Moxie remarked about how much she enjoyed visiting Kirk's shop.

"I appreciate your compliments on our selection of spices from around the world, too. You are coming to coffee hour in fellowship hall now, aren't you?"

Moxie looked at Matt, and Matt looked at Moxie. "Shall we?"

Matt said he was planning on going. He brought his latest baking accomplishment and he said, "This fellow here, Kirk, is always a great taste tester."

"Oh, I'd be honored once again," said the kitchen shop owner.

As they walked into the bustling fellowship hall, Moxie recognized a few others among the crowd as business owners or sales assistants she'd seen about town on her previous visits. The salesclerk from All Dun Up, the clothing store where she got the clothes she was wearing, was among them.

Matt proceeded to the coffee urn and got two cups of coffee and a couple of his muffins he had set out, while Moxie became engaged in a conversation with a shopkeeper about moving to the community and the need to find a suitable place to live.

"I don't mean to interrupt. Here you go," Matt said handing Moxie her coffee and muffin.

"Excuse me, I'm going to grab something for myself and head out. Nice to meet you Moxie. See you around, Matt."

Matt and Moxie moved over to a nearby table and remained standing. "Tell the chef what you think of his cooking."

"Tastes quite a bit like the Morning Glory's muffins."

"Yes. They are my Morning Glory muffins."

"Are you the person behind the Morning Glory muffins over at the restaurant?"

"Yes, I've been freelancing my baking for a long time."

"This batch has a tweak to them. I enhanced them with a little Sunday sunshine twist. All kinds of wholesome things and a few secrets to kick up the appeal."

Moxie took another bite, this time paying closer attention. Her eyes widened. "Oh, you can make me a batch of these anytime, Matt! "What is it, what's the secret??"

"I'm not giving away my secret ingredient, not even to you Moxie."

"Fair, enough."

"Glad you like them. I am just getting started! I've got killer culinary skills I need to begin rolling out as soon as the time is right."

"Well, I always knew you could make a respectable donut. You've added much finesse to your baking skills."

"Oh, I've got a lot more in my pocket beyond pastry skills, Moxie."

"Oh, really! Then you really were busy in the years we lost touch, weren't you?"

When the coffee hour was nearly over, someone banged on a table across the room. It was the pastor. "Ok, before you all leave, there is something you need to tell me. I am assuming the muffins in parchment paper cups, sitting in a basket, were made by the fella in town who makes the Morning Glory muffins for the breakfast place by the same name. I'm awed at how good they are and wonder why they taste slightly different and even better than ever."

Kirk, the kitchen shop owner spoke up. "Yay,

Matt. Hey Rev, he's trying to earn his passage into heaven." Laughter spread through the crowd. "His enhanced recipe is out of this world. I'm still trying to figure out the intermingling of complex flavors. A pinch of cardamom and something else, maybe?"

"Thanks, buddy!" Matt said, his gaze fixing on Kirk from across the room. "A high mark coming from you is valuable. Someday, I might ask you to jot down your recommendation down on paper!"

"Will do!" Kirk said, giving Matt the thumbs up.

Matt helped take down tables and store away chairs while Moxie helped some women clean up the coffee station and kitchen as she made more new acquaintances. When the fellowship hall was sparkling, he and Moxie got ready to head out with the other stragglers.

Just before leaving a woman came and introduced herself. "I understand you are moving to this community. I just wanted to say welcome. You'll like it here. We need more people like you. I understand you were the one who gave us all the provisions for our last meeting." Moxie nodded.

"Well, thank you."

"And thanks for reaching out to meet me," said Moxie.

"See you around, I gotta run and get back to my store."

“So, what’s next Moxie? Anything else you want to do while you are in Belle Aire today?”

“Let’s walk up town just for a minute. Other than that, I’m good – I could head on home and be perfectly satisfied with doing nothing else for the rest of the day.”

They walked past the stationery store to the bookstore. “Hold up, Matt. I want to stop here to grab the complimentary weekly rag sheet The Junction Jabber.”

“You’ve got it!”

Moxie grabbed two copies, and handed one to Matt.

A woman was propping open the bookstore door with her foot and trying to move the newspaper rack outside at the same time, “Wait a minute. I’ll help you,” said Matt. He put his newspaper under his arm and grabbed the rack and placed it on the stoop.

“Thanks, Matt.”

“Didn’t we just see you? How did you get down here so quickly?” asked Moxie.

The woman shrugged her shoulders.

"You’re Jane, right?”

“Yes, I am owner of this bookstore, Words that Heal.”

Moxie said again how nice it was to meet her and then goodbye till next time. She and Matt proceeded back to her car parked at the church. She unlocked the car and Matt opened the door for her.

"You'll make it for the next the community dinner, won't you?"

"Sure Matt, if I can think of something to bring that I won't be embarrassed to feed other people.

"It's not about that Moxie. All this crowd really cares about is a chance to gather. Food will be plentiful, as it always is. Just join in."

"Wait, Matt, don't rush me off. I need to tell you something. I saw Johanna in the pews this morning, but as far as I know she didn't stay afterward. I've made a decision. I am joining you and Johanna in this new venture you two are pulling together. My answer is yes."

Matt hugged her. "You don't know how happy I am to hear that."

Chapter 15

"So, IT SOUNDS LIKE we three are in agreement!" Johanna said standing on the front porch of #48 Union.

"I think we've discussed every inch of this property right down to the flooring underlayment, right Matt?" asked Moxie. They had discussed the potential use of each room and the common spaces in relation to their overall plan. Matt and Moxie agreed to live on premises each taking a bedroom in the wing off the main house containing a two-bedroom apartment. In the end it was decided it would make life so much easier, and if all went according to plan, that would mean no moving twice.

Moxie was so grateful when Beverly said, "The usage of the 2nd floor apartment in the sewing shop building is still undecided, so there was no hurry for you to vacate." Beverly was happy to continue to rent to Moxie for three more months until the closing of #48 Union.

"Matt and Moxie, I hope you'll take my advice. This project needs to go one step at a time, so it's not too much too soon and we don't get overwhelmed. Once we see success in one area, we will take on the next step and add to what's working."

"That makes so much sense. Especially given the nature of the beast. A new venture with a bit of a make it up as we go along."

"Let's keep that between us, shall we Matt?" Moxie snickered.

"So, Mr. Realtor, soon-to-be what? Art/Creative/Wellness Center Food and Beverage Manager or Head of Culinary Arts?

"Head of Culinary Arts. I kind of like that," said Johanna.

"Me, too. What's next to secure this place as ours?" asked Moxie. "Do we know all systems are a go? The elevator, the roof, the electrical, plumbing and heating?"

"Not quite. We need property inspections. I'll arrange for that," said Matt. "And we need to secure this space with a deposit and intent to buy agreement."

"I will work directly with Loyal, your attorney on organization of the non-profit and the financial aspects of it. Matt's attorney and your respective bankers and the silent partner will all be part of those discussions and decisions, so everything is fair, equitable and satisfies the needs of all parties involved," said Johanna.

Matt and Moxie looked at each other. "I'm greatly relieved to hear you say that."

"Me, too, Moxie!" said Matt.

"I am going to give you both a number of important tasks. Brainstorm names and taglines for this creative women's art center we've been envisioning. Divvy up who will oversee the responsibilities of various duties and what your official titles will be. Will you need assistance in the way of employees or volunteers from the get-go or can we hold off on adding staff?"

"Matt," asked Johanna, "once we get the place inspected, we should have a better idea of a timeline for settlement and opening, shouldn't we?"

"Correct," Matt said, nodding yes.

"I sure am happy this place is partially furnished and almost turn-key," said Moxie. I'm kind of regretting I jumped to get rid of Eunice and Mildred's furnishings and other items so quickly."

"Oh Moxie, don't regret that. New beginnings, remember? Besides, you had no way of knowing what was going to transpire."

"No, I didn't. I had to do something with their enormous stash of collectibles, bric-a-brac and tchotchkes. Whatever you want to call them. Man, that sure was a sore point between them!"

"Was it? I thought all women liked their geegaws," said Matt.

"Oh, the contention came with not using the right terminology and their different preferences."

"What do you mean?" asked Johanna.

Eunice often rubbed Mildred the wrong way when it came to discussing collectibles. She'd say, "I don't have doo-dads, Eunice. What I have are fine quality bibelots. And please don't call them my tchotchkes. They are far from being one in the same."

"The first time I heard the two women's banter about collectibles, I was surprised. Although it was apparent Mildred was used to the finer things in life, never ever did she act like an elitist, but Eunice saw things differently. 'Oh, for Pete's Sake, Mildred, you'd think you were a Waterford crystal figurine on display up on a rosewood pedestal when you talk like that! Who do you think you are? God almighty?'"

Moxie continued. "I had a sneaking suspicion it was a running battle Mildred and Eunice enjoyed between themselves, and they liked keeping the argument going. It was comical to hear them go at it back and forth."

"How could we ever forget those two women?" Johanna asked, already knowing the answer.

"Some of their furniture probably would

have fit the era of this building. But, again, I am going to advise you not to go out and buy anything at the start. Some of these rooms will be sparse until the place is fully operational and by then we will have a better handle on what we need. Start-up marketing, signage, a small bit of schwag will be wise initial investments in the business. And Matt, you will probably need some kitchen gear to get started. Again, we will start with limited food offerings for our participants. Remember we will be a non-profit so we may be able to get donations from the community and other sources to fill some of our initial needs. That's what we've already discussed, right?"

"Yep, we need to be resourceful," said Matt. Moxie nodded her approval because she had the feeling Matt was not quite as used to scrimping and making do as she was.

"Kirk has already voiced his desire to help out with kitchen supplies."

"Great! I've been doing this long enough to have my pulse on a lot of other resources and connections to help us out."

"Well, are we done for today? I'd like to lock this place up. I need to get back to the office and work on scheduling the inspections."

"Matt, keep me posted as to what kind of

deposit we need to come up with, and I'll work with the people I mentioned earlier."

"Moxie, brainstorm away and begin to think about our programs here at the women's creative center. I hope you two are as excited as I am!"

"Indeed!" said Matt.

"I'm so looking forward to seeing what we can make of this place and our vision for it." said Moxie, as she looked at her surroundings.

Chapter 16

IT WAS GETTING HARDER and harder to be patient. Moxie had heard and seen hide nor hair from Matt or Johanna. At the risk of being a nag, she didn't call or email them. Last time the three had been together Johanna had given each a "to-do list." The tasks on Matt and Johanna's lists such as dealing with banks and attorneys in organizing a non-profit and scheduling appointments for various inspections always took longer than expected.

The waiting game that came with certain life situations was always a tough pill to swallow. *Easier said than done*, thought Moxie. Trying to be patient waiting for the next job to come along when Matt had fired her at the donut shop taught Moxie that sometimes the wait is worth it. That was when Moxie's job at the sewing shop came along. When she was lamenting the loss, Mildred called her up nearly every morning. “Have you taken your daily vitamins today?” she'd ask Moxie. The first time Mildred asked her, Moxie told her she that doesn't take any. “But dear, you must enrich yourself with prayer and faith. And don’t let Eunice tell you otherwise. She says her daily nourishment comes from a chocolate kiss with her coffee first thing in the morning. Yet, those sweet treats always get her into trouble. Once she starts...well, you know as well as I do what happens.”

Moxie decided to put her faith into action and not call her cohorts. Besides, “No news is good news,” she kept telling herself. So, she put her energy into doing what Johanna asked her to do. She had made a healthy list of potential names for the art/wellness center. It was going to be interesting to see what Matt came up with. Since Matt's forte was not with running any kind of creative business, he said he'd leave program scheduling to Moxie and defer to her choices. But he voiced his opinion that the art/creativity/wellness center ought to have a culinary arts component to it. Moxie agreed whole-heartedly and told Matt she'd let him know when she was ready for his input into that aspect.

Moxie felt like she’d hit paydirt when she placed an ad through a couple of social media platforms stating “Going Out of Business: Upholstery fabric and upholstery trim for sale. Perfect for start-up business!" Everything was snatched up so quickly, she said to herself, *I know that was you God, thank you very much!* Matt would be so proud of how quickly she solved the puzzle of what to do with it, and she was pleased she wasn't going to have to rely on Matt to help her. He had enough on his to-do list since he was still working in real estate. How many other clients was he trying to work with?

Moxie's introduction to members of the Neighbor-to-Neighbor-Network was fast tracked as she put together programming for the creative center. Matt gave her all the necessary names and contact information so she could send out a letter rallying members to the cause. It appeared from the responses there had been a groundswell of interest for such an endeavor long before Moxie got involved. Several members stated they'd been looking for the right people to head up such an organization for quite some time.

Moxie was not going to let any doubt creep into her whether she was up to being the Program Director or not. Their official titles were still up for discussion, but that's what she called herself. Johanna's assurance that the necessary resources would be in place took away much worry knowing the higher being would work out the details.

Well, what's next on my list? Moxie thought. The stack of mail sitting in front of her was nagging. She opened the envelope on top whose return Post Office Box number she didn't recognize and read the first line "We are sorry to inform you the elevator at #48 Union Street has failed inspection. For further information on how to rectify the situation, please contact the department supervisor." At the bottom of the correspondence, it indicated carbon copies had been mailed to Johanna and Matt.

Moxie was floored! She looked skyward, *now what Lord, now what?*

Just then the phone rang. It was Matt.

"Well, hello! A fine day it is!" From the chipper tone in his voice Matt obviously hadn't opened his copy of the letter.

"Yeah, right!" Moxie was having a hard time finding a bright spot in the skies overhead. "Matt, have you gotten the correspondence about the elevator inspection?"

"Yes, I have. And I just got off the phone with Johanna."

"So now what?"

"We'll deal with it."

"But what if the repair will be extensive? What if we..."

"Hold up. Hold up, Moxie. Please don't throw

all the what ifs at me when we don’t even know what the problem is. Set it in your mind right now to think only of what you want the outcome to be, not what you don't want. Got it?”

“Yeah, I guess.”

“See it as already ours! In the meantime, I'm hunting down the facts, and Johanna is checking into her resources. We've got several issues in other areas too. Some could be costly, but we don’t know yet.”

“So, what am I supposed to do?”

“No freaking out on me. Moxie, do you hear me? Keep making headway with your to-do list. We will get back to you.”

“Ok. If you say so.”

That night when Moxie went to bed, she set her intentions on what she wanted. Her last thought as she drifted off to sleep were the words of Miss Mildred “If God gives you a vision that does not meet your budget, he’s not checking on your bank account, he’s checking your faith.”

Chapter 17

"OK, ARE YOU ALL READY?" asked Matt. Moxie had set the kitchen table with the likes of which Miss Mildred would have been proud even though the gathering was not social, but a business luncheon. Miss Mildred always said, "Set a table as if you're having the last supper with your best goblet and all."

Isn't this nice having Matt, Johanna, Reverend Thad Bridges with me at the table? thought Moxie, as they all took their seats.

The theologian in the group said how much he enjoyed gathering at the table in different people's homes. "You know, it's been said, the oldest form of theatre is at the dinner table. I don't think the adage came from a famous biblical leader, but its worthy of consideration."

"Macha tea lattes, chicken salad with apples, walnuts and sunflower seeds on a bed of romaine, a side of dates stuffed with cream cheese with a toasted pecan on top, and we will end with green tea chiffon cake, how's that?" Matt asked, not waiting for an answer. "This tea was chosen for a detox. To give us immunity from negative thoughts and recycling old ideas. Let's roll!"

"Who would like to do the honors of opening this meeting?" asked Moxie.

"I will! If I may be so bold," said Reverend Bridges. He bowed his head and the others followed. "Dear God, thank you for the entrepreneurial spirits gathered around this table. Give us the guidance and positive energy we need to work hard and make this new enterprise prosperous, abundant, and a gift to others."

Four "Amens" were heard around the table.

Johanna spoke up next. "So, Matt and I have a lot to share with you, but we will spare you all the details and sum it up and tell you where things stand now. The inspections detected some electrical and plumbing issues. They can be easily remedied without too much cost. Overall, this place is in good condition. However, the elevator is kaput, basically."

Moxie looked around the table at everyone's expression. All had a cool and collected appearance as if the only one bothered by the news was her. "So, that means we need to have a new elevator installed. More costly than we anticipated between the parts and the labor. I have been exploring ways to get funding and I think I have come up with a solution. Now hear me out, Moxie. We need you to help us with this."

"Ok. How, Johanna?"

"By giving a presentation to the Neighbor-to-Neighbor-Network and a few others."

Oh, heaven help me, Moxie thought but she didn't voice her thoughts. *A presentation?* Moxie swallowed hard. As much as she tried not to spew it, a "but" slipped out. She'd never done any public speaking.

"Here's the deal," said the Reverend. He turned to look Moxie square in the eye. "There is no need to be anxious. Do this as naturally as possible. Just open your heart and give a personal testimony about why we need this creative art center and how it will serve the community and beyond. Try not to rehearse. God will give you the words you need, have faith."

Moxie thought about the book Mildred had authored, and she said the same thing about where her words came from.

Matt and Johanna spoke up. "Moxie, you can do this! We know you can." Moxie sat quietly trying to keep a cooperative attitude.

"Well, when do you want me to do this?"

"Tomorrow morning on Zoom," said Johanna. "It will not ALL be on your shoulders. We are just looking for your testimony. Then I will follow up with particulars regarding what we need financially to swing the center into gear. It does not matter where or who the funds come from."

"And I am looking for community collaboration with the creative programs." said Moxie. "But more about that later."

Damn those piercing blue eyes, Moxie thought. Matt seemed to be looking right through her. No one said anything else, the other two looked down at the table.

"May I please be excused? I need to use the lady's room." All nodded their heads. Moxie went to the bathroom closed the door, leaned up against it and slid down until she was sitting on the floor, not lingering long. She got up, splashed water on her face and looked in the mirror repeating the words of a social media motivational guru she'd heard that very morning. "...you are stronger than your struggles and more fierce than your fears." She said it a second time to herself, sealing it in her brain.

Moxie opened the door and walked boldly to the table. "Ok, I'll do it!"

"Yes!" Three cheers went up in the room.

"So, can we meet here at seven tomorrow

morning?" Johanna asked. "There's more privacy here than other places. Bring your computers, everyone, as insurance. You know how technology can be squirrely, then we will have backups. Matt assured everyone he had a Zoom account and was adept at using it. "I've already sent out an invitation to key people."

"Wait, you already sent out the invitation?" Moxie asked with surprised tone.

"Yes, I didn't say who the headliner would be. I just posed it as an informational meeting. I want to go live before NNN members open for business so they will all tune in."

"So, that concludes our meeting today," said Johanna. "One step at a time and then we move to the next."

"Am I allowed to ask a question?"

"Of course, Moxie. Fire away," said Matt.

"What should I wear?"

"You women! It's always the first question, isn't it? Moxie, what's wrong with what you have on now?" Matt asked. "People are more interested in what you have to say than the other."

"Thanks, Matt." She liked how she looked in her new outfit from one of the boutiques in Belle Aire. That is why she'd chosen it for that day's meeting.

"Moxie, we have one task for you first thing in the morning. We have lots of space now that your sewing gear is out of here. See what you can do to arrange a corner of this big room that we can broadcast from."

"Will we need chairs, or will I be standing?" Moxie inquired.

"Now that you asked, how would you feel if you and I sat together and made it more informal like we are having a friend-to-friend conversation?"

"Oh, that would be great!" Johanna aired more final thoughts. "I'll bring a few pieces of different kinds of art to decorate the walls behind us, and perhaps you have a quilt or other fiber art you'd like to include. We will have time to hang it before we go live."

"Matt, bring your tools!" said the Reverend.

Johanna had an ulterior motive behind her request to get the room ready for the Zoom broadcast. She was hoping the task would keep Moxie busy and not thinking about what she was going to say.

"Well, thank you for agreeing to share your personal story with the community tomorrow, Moxie. Those who have a vested interest will be watching from up above. I just know it!" the Reverend said, looking skyward.

Chapter 18

Moxie had risen at 5 a.m., not to work on her presentation, but to put finishing touches on two wall hangings she hoped to complete before she and Johanna went live on Zoom. She still had her sewing machine and some basic sewing supplies, so she was able to work on the task which had been put on hold for a long time, and she was able to complete it. The wall hangings would add credence to her plea. Somehow Moxie just knew it.

Two hours later when Matt, Johanna and Rev. Bridges arrived, Moxie had coffee brewing in her new coffeemaker. She'd finally done away with Eunice's ancient stove top percolator and gotten herself a programable drip coffee maker.

The place became a beehive of activity. Matt had brought some of his Morning Glory muffins to sustain them. Before Moxie knew it, Matt and

Reverend Bridges had the technology hooked up and it was time to go live.

"Let's roll," said Matt, as Johanna and Moxie took their two seats in front of the computer screen.

Johanna spoke first by welcoming everyone who was joining in. She introduced herself and the newcomer to the Neighbor-to-Neighbor-Network, Moxie, and then let her take over from there.

Moxie stood briefly from her chair. "We are here this morning because of these two women, Mildred Millicent and Eunice Easterbook. Moxie pointed to the two 18 x 24" fabric portrait wall hangings behind her she had stitched and sewn.

Then she sat back down next to Johanna. "Before I met those two women, and many of you knew and loved them, I was a ragged and torn individual whose life needed to be mended. My life was a mess, to put it plainly. But I am not the only woman they helped. We want to honor Mildred and Eunice's legacy by starting an art wellness center for women who are struggling to find their way in the world. As for me, finding my passion for the fiber arts, which Mildred and Eunice introduced me to, has made an enormous difference in my life. My life will never be the same thanks to their threads of character shaping that are woven in every fiber of my being and the love for an art form. Pick your passion – pottery, painting, writing, culinary creation, drawing, basketmaking, weaving, jewelry making – any kind of art heals. There are women in this community and in the great beyond who need to discover and explore themselves through art."

Moxie went on to briefly state the kinds of programs they hoped to bring to the community. "We've found a great centrally located property for this endeavor. But we are facing just a few challenges, and I will let Johanna speak with you about that."

Johanna briefly outlined the ways that community can be involved in supporting the project and how much funding was necessary to replace the elevator and open the doors. "At the end of this presentation we will post our contact information. Please get in touch if you'd like to be involved in this exciting venture into healing people, Neighbor-to-Neighbor creatively.

She continued, "I'd like to end this presentation with a quote from Julia Cameron who once said, "*Creativity is God's gift to us. Using our creativity is our gift back to God.*" What's stopping you from giving whatever personal resources you may have for our community's wellness?"

When the presentation was over, Moxie, let out a huge sigh of relief. Her three cohorts came over and hugged her.

"You were brilliant Moxie!" said Johanna.

Moxie couldn't move out of her seat. It had taken all she had. "Honestly, I don't even know what I said. The words, they just kind of came out of nowhere and took over."

"Hey Rev, your suggestion of ending with the Julia Cameron quote was a great one! We will see what happens," said Matt.

"Yes, Reverend Bridges, thanks for your good advice," said Moxie.

"Moxie, please, may we drop the formality? Call me Thad or Pastor Thad."

Moxie smiled broadly. "Thanks, Thad."

It didn't take long for the phone to start ringing and emails started to arrive in Johanna's mailbox. Besides promises of financial support, the garden center offered to maintain the lawns and extensive gardens at #48 Union, the bookstore wanted to give workshops on basic bookbinding, the hair salon was interested in giving healthy hair workshops, a women's clothing boutique offered presentations on how to color coordinate an outfit to create mood. The local sheep farm was interested in demonstrating yarn spinning. Calls from local artists who wanted to give beginner's workshops, non-gratis, in their field of expertise came quickly, and Moxie's programs for the first half of the year rounded out nicely.

A few weeks later, a small package came in the mail from the local stationery store, Parchment Papers. It was gold sealing wax, and an embossing stamp like what they used in letter writing back in yesteryear. The stamp was of a heart with the words "*The Creative*" above it. A beautiful notecard accompanied which said, "Here is a check to help you seal the deal. Please put it toward the new elevator so you can open the women's art center. Please look forward to our participation in other ways." Other big financial support came from numerous organizations whom they had invited to the Zoom presentation, but no one was aware they were watching. Blessings, more than any could ever have fathomed, poured in. Proof that Moxie had gotten to the heart of the matter.

Chapter 19

"THAT'S IT!" said Matt as he hammered the last nail for the second of the two fiber art portraits Moxie had stitched of Mildred and Eunice. "Our figureheads are now framed and hung!"

"The frame shop in town sure did a wonderful job, didn't they, Matt?"

"Yes, the frame accentuates the art beautifully."

Moxie had stenciled on the plaster wall above the portraits Miss Eunice's infamous words, using a bold Bookman Old Style font,

Rules of the house ~ If you don't know what you are doing, just fudge it!

"God, you come up with some great ideas, Moxie. I especially like the quote because if things go like we anticipate most people who walk through these doors will be beginners. People who want to explore with art and are not necessarily in it to become professionals. They want to have fun, discover, meet like-minded individuals and most importantly soothe the stresses of life."

"You know Matt, the house rules apply to us too. Let this be a joyful, playful endeavor not something to raise the blood pressure."

"Amen to that," said Matt earnestly. "And let's make a promise right here, right now. One morsel of dark chocolate every morning with coffee to set the day right."

Moxie looked at Matt with mischievous eyes. "Nah, I've got an even better idea."

"Ok, then, bring it on. What say you?" That's what Moxie appreciated about Matt. He was never threatened by a woman's opinion or someone's suggestions which may override his. He was all ears and had an open heart.

"A candy dish right at the door filled to the brim all the live-long day filled with your homemade truffles. So, anyone can partake of those antioxidants any time, day or night."

"All the live-long day, huh? Where did you get that expression?"

"Where do you think?" Matt moved over close to Moxie and raised his hand, she raised hers to meet his. They did a high five slap of the hands and then embraced in a friendly warm hug. "Deal," they said at the same time.

"Say, what time is it? How much time do we have before the NNN group arrives? Are you ready?"

"Me? I'm not even stressing. I'm just gonna do what I did before. Speak from the heart. It worked, didn't it? Look at the grants and other support we've gotten. All those folks who said they'd rather honor Mildred and Eunice in some way rather than sitting through a memorial service the two ladies didn't want anyway, sure have pulled through."

"I'm excited to see the reaction of our NNN members to what we've planned for them today, Moxie."

An hour later twelve familiar faces showed up at the door together, the same twelve that had made their move to #48 so effortless. There was no need to hire a moving company, between several trucks and vans and lots of helping hands from the NNN, move-in day was not nearly as traumatic as Moxie thought it would be. She hated it when her mind turned molehills into mountains. Something Matt said she was good at.

"Come in, come in!" Moxie said, welcoming everyone. After a few opening remarks similar to what Moxie said over Zoom, Matt handed out baskets to each of them and led them outside behind the building. Last time you all were here on move-in day we were so busy hauling boxes and such I didn't get to show you our little Eden behind the building. Wait till you see it and the spring flowers! They are beautiful."

"What are the baskets for?" someone from the crowd asked.

"Each one of you pick out two small rocks, no boulders, please and you'll see once we are inside what we are going to do with them. I also want you to pick some posies from our gardens. We've got plenty to spare so enjoy! Don't be bashful."

When they were finished with the backyard tour, which seemed to impress everyone, Matt said, "Let's proceed indoors. You can leave your baskets on the hall table for later. Put your flowers in the containers of water we have set out. We have the morning jammed packed with activity, but we will get you out of here before lunch so you can return to your businesses.

"First, I want to give you a quick tour inside now that we are all settled and there aren't boxes stacked everywhere. The tour will end in the kitchen where your first creative experiential workshop will begin. And you'll be making chocolate truffles to take home."

"Yeah, if they last until we get out the door!"

some wise guy said. After the thought was voiced, Matt knew who it came from - Pastor Thad.

"Get Your Creative On!" Moxie said as she passed out logoed aprons which also had the tag line *For the Health of Community* on each of them. The next hour was spent making easy delicious treats. Matt explained how if they wanted to up their game, they could take the basic recipe he had handed out and experiment with it at home. "Use different flavorings like a little orange essence or decorative sprinkles or finely chopped nuts as topping to suit your hearts desires." The group worked diligently, some quicker than those who were not as comfortable with being hands-on in a kitchen.

"Ok, now that we're finished with this creative experience, I hope you enjoyed it. On to the next. Moxie is waiting for you in the front parlor to the left of the big winding staircase. Stop and pick up your rocks from your baskets."

When all twelve had arrived in front of Moxie, she said, "Ok. This workshop is a win-win for both of us. I'd encourage you to creatively incorporate the name of your business or organization somewhere on one of the rocks we are going to paint and put the name of this organization on the second. The idea is for you to leave the rock with the name of your business in our garden where it can be seen. While in town, hopefully, people will become curious after seeing your rock and come visit your business. Remember, we are expecting non-community members or visitors to town for several day art retreats once we are fully geared up. The second rock, with the name of this organization on it, we'd greatly appreciate it if you'd take it back to your place of business and put it by your cash register or use it for a door stop this summer at the entrance, or put it in a noticeable place to help us promote our art wellness center. Other than that, no rights or wrongs, no self-judgement. Remember if you don't know what you are doing, fudge it! Play away. You have 45 minutes, and by the size of your rocks, you should be able to finish. We don't expect anyone to become the next Roberto Rizzo, as first-time rock painters."

When they were finished, it was Moxie's turn to lead again. "Last of all, we are going to do a real quicky. A "faux stained glass type project," using a few of your favorite flowers from your basket. We will mostly be incorporating the colorful flowerhead to make pressed flower bookmarks or window light catchers. Sorry to disappoint you, this is not exactly Tiffany quality stuff. This is an activity you could do with children, mind you. But it's still fun and made by pressing your flowers between two pieces of waxed paper and gently ironing it. And then we will trim them nicely and add a little extra embellishment to give it a finished look. You can either take your creation home or if you decide to make a bookmark, you can leave it here. We plan on using the corner of one of our upstairs rooms as a nook for art and craft books. We've had a generous donation from our community to do so."

When the activity was over, Moxie said, "The other flowers in your basket take home or back to your place of business and try your hand at a little flower arranging or give them out at the end of the day to build a little good will with your employees."

Matt appeared with the truffles from the kitchen and handed the beautifully boxed sweets to each attendee on their way out the door. Moxie wrapped the flower stems in wet paper towels and put them in plastic bags to keep them from drooping.

Kirk from the kitchen shop was last to leave. "I sure hope those who work in town will take advantage of the opportunities here because it will make for happier Main Street shopkeepers and their crew. If it benefits one, it benefits all."

When everyone had gone, Matt turned to Moxie, "Feeling pretty good?"

"Yeah, I am. Overall, I think it went well. The real test will come when we open the doors to people we don't know, not knowing what we are really in for!"

Chapter 20

THE SMALL DETAILS! Moxie thought, as she and Matt prepared for opening day which was scheduled about a month after hosting the NNN for a soft opening. In retrospect it was a good thing they gave themselves another four weeks because the last-minute to-do list was much longer than either of them expected. And for a while it seemed as if for every item on the list they ticked off, another was added.

Once the hand carved wooden sign went up stating *Get Your Creative On: For the Health of Community* by-passing cars kept tooting. The day Reverend Thad came to call to see if they needed help, he said, "I'm not deaf to what I am hearing. Listen to that! You've got angels heralding the upcoming opening of this place with blaring horns."

At first Moxie and Matt thought it was only

NNN members, but then they began to suspect it was other people, too. The toots exceeded twelve on the first day the sign appeared and had continued off and on each day. They hoped their visibility factor on social media would be good too, and their following would grow beyond all expectations.

The website was up and running and there had been an encouraging number of inquiries daily. The completed on-line registrations along with the required deposits were beginning to come in. "Thank the Lord, let all the blessings flow," said Reverend Thad.

Johanna had suggested starting first with half day and full day workshops. For the first three months, she said many quirks will still be needed to be worked out, so schedule being open for business only two days a week. "And don't worry. We've got to begin somewhere and it's best that what you provide is of good quality rather than shabbily stitched together. Gain your clientele's confidence so they return time and time again and help spread the word. We will only actively promote locally, until you are both comfortable with opening the range and depth of our target marketing." Frankly, Matt and Moxie were happy, not disappointed, to hear this from Johanna.

One morning, approximately two weeks from

the first real day of business the phone rang. It was a woman eager to register for opening day and attend the full day of workshops.

Moxie asked the woman's name so she could schedule her in.

"My name?" There was a long pause as if the woman had forgotten who she was. "Oh, sorry. Adalyte."

Unique, thought Moxie. "Can you spell that for me?"

"Sure.... A-D-A- -L-Y-T-E."

"How about your last name?"

"That's all I go by."

The woman didn't seem too forthcoming with details but sounded pleasant enough. Now, I'm going to need the account number on your credit card so we can charge the workshop fees. The woman read each digit carefully. How about the expiration date?" Moxie asked.

"Mine? Never. I hope to be eternal."

Don't we all? thought Moxie but she didn't air it. Instead, she clarified, "No, the card's expiration date."

"Oh, that. Here," the woman slowly read the expiration date to Moxie as if struggling."

"One more detail. The bank can be sticklers, so give me your full name exactly as it reads on your credit or debit card."

"Let me see," said the lady. "There's a reflection making it hard for me to read. Oh, here, now I can see it easier, Celeste B. Bright."

Moxie had to hold in her laugh. Is this lady for real? "Celeste is that C-E-L-E-S-T-E?"

"Yes. Yes, that's right."

"Is it B-R-I-G-H-T or B-R-I-T-E."

"The first way you spelled it B-R-I-G-H-T. I've always been grateful for that. It sounds less trendy, don't you think? Not like here today, gone tomorrow."

Then Moxie proceeded to take down her address which happened to be a Post Office Box in town.

"Oh, a local! Great!" Moxie said, "Have you been here long?"

"Yes, but I don't get out and about much. My night life is such that I sleep a good part of the day."

"Now let me give you your total and your confirmation number of your reserved spot. That total includes light morning and mid-afternoon refreshments along with a delicious lunch. And of course, your art workshops."

"Oh, fine, fine. Any price one needs to pay to get into heaven makes it worth it. I've been waiting for a long, long time to do something like this. I'm so looking forward to it."

"We are too! So, we will see you two weeks from now! And I have your email, so I will send you a written confirmation also."

"Thanks for your help," the woman said cheerfully and hung up.

That evening after all work was done, Matt threw together a quick taco salad. Moxie and Matt sat having dinner together visiting in their living quarters.

"So, how was your day, Moxie?"

"Well...fine. I got a lot done. Our storefront point-of-sale equipment got tested today. We had our first phone registration. The rest of the registrations have been through e-commerce. But I must say the telephone conversation was interesting."

"How so?"

Moxie tried to explain without being judgmental and without a word for word recounting of the conversation. She didn't know why. Matt had mentioned he'd heard it all and seen it all as far as women go after living with six sisters. *Perhaps*, thought Moxie, *from being with Eunice and Mildred, my perception of people is hypersensitive or a bit skewed*. Perhaps Adalyte or Celeste B. Bright wasn't strange at all. Moxie looked forward to meeting her.

"Sounds like her personality is either electric or eccentric! Say no more, Moxie. I get it. The woman was like a chip off the old chocolate block. A relative of Eunice, only different?"

"Yep! You got it Matt. Enough to melt a heart." The two had a good laugh.

Chapter 21

SEVEN OF THE EIGHT opening day participants arrived and parked. They were standing getting to know one another out on the big front porch at #48 Union. Most of them looked to be women of an age trying to establish their "Next Act or Questors." A friendly yet quiet group they were. Some seemed a little nervous. They talked with Matt and Moxie about the day's agenda. After a brief introduction, they would go to the kitchen and make truffles, just as Matt had done with the NNN group. He discovered a way to shorten the workshop through advanced prep to leave time for the other lengthier sessions of the day.

Finally, when the last car drove in the parking lot, Matt sighed relief. The woman exited her car quickly and joined the others on the porch.

"Hello! You must be Adalyte or is it Celeste? What would you prefer to be called?" asked Moxie.

When her pudgy cheeks rose to smile her eyes made crescent moons. Her short, dark-as-night hair spiked upward toward the sky. The tips of her hair were as if they had just met with the bleach bottle. Moxie observed a few of the participants wide-eyed reactions to the woman, but Moxie never blinked. After all, in the past her hair had been every color in the rainbow, literally and regrettably!

"As of today, I am in a new phase, so call me Celeste. Adalyte makes me sound too dim."

"Well, welcome Celeste. We are glad you have joined us." Moxie had each one in the group introduce themselves.

"Well, into the kitchen we go!" said Matt leading the way.

As they walked Moxie explained to Celeste what she'd said to the others. The first workshop was truffle making. That way, the kitchen would then be freed up for the rest of the day for Matt and his food prep for the breaks and lunch. Matt was able to convince a new part-time kitchen assistant from John Peter's Pub down the street to help him whenever she was available. Nice young kid Rebecca was, and she appreciated the fact that she could add the experience to her resume.

When the group arrived in the kitchen and gathered around Matt to hear instructions, Celeste, who was standing at the center front of the group said, "Wait a minute." She reached down between the ruffled placket of her primarily blue paisley silk blouse and fished around down in her cleavage. Then she drew her necklace out from underneath her shirt, so it was visible. The necklace appeared hand-crafted and costly intertwined with all sorts of silver charms, multicolored glass beads and slim silk ribbons running throughout. Celeste reached behind her neck to the clasp. "There now!" she said out loud. "I've set my intentions." The star-shaped glass beads interwoven among all the round and oblong ones began twinkling around the necklace.

"Well, alrighty then. It's time to start!" said Matt. The next hour was spent making the truffles and then leaving them to cool so they could be boxed up. As they were finishing up, several women exclaimed what fun the activity was, and they were so happy to learn the chocolate truffles would be taken home to enjoy. Matt then led the group up the winding staircase to the largest upper room, where an instructor from the local Pottery Shed was all set up for a session of hand-building with clay.

"Hello, have a seat wherever you'd like. My name is Justine. I work at the Pottery Shed.

How is everyone today? How was your chocolate making?"

Celeste spoke up the loudest. "Just call me Queen Godiva or QG, if that's easier. I know becoming a professional chocolatier is in my future." You could hear snickers in the room.

"Has anyone done any hand-building with clay before?"

No one had, so they were all starting out on ground level. Justine explained some of tools and then showed some examples of hand-built pottery. "Today, we are going to be making hand coiled bowls, raku fired." She went on to explain what raku was and how firing using combustibles such as sawdust in a kiln outside (such as in a large barrel) is possible. "We haven't decided whether to fire your pieces here or down at the Pottery Shed. It will be next week or the week after. I will send you each an email with the details so if anyone is interested in seeing the raku firing process, come watch. It's an education in itself. In the meantime, I will take care to handle your bowls as they need to be kept for the firing."

The morning proceeded smoothly, and by the looks on the women's faces, they were all enjoying what they were doing. A mid-morning break served in one corner of the room brought refreshment of fruit smoothies and Matt's Morning Glory and Vanilla Chai muffins.

A visitor, Rev. Athalia, or Athie as she liked to be called, Pastor Bridges assistant, stopped in. She went from table to table with the instructor seeing everyone's work. As Reverend Athie walked, she hummed. Passing by Deborah, a workshop attendee, Deborah began to sing the lyrics, "With this art, I give my heart. Help me see, what it shall be."

When the instructor Justine got to Celeste , she said, "Move over Mike Helke. Another star is on her way!" Celeste looked at Justine blankly.

At the end of the two-hour session, Moxie left her office to look at the women's pottery creations. "We will take an hour's lunch break now. A vegan option will be available," Moxie told the participants.

Lunch went well, everyone seemed to enjoy visiting with one another and Matt's food. Besides expanding his repertoire of recipes, Moxie couldn't help but notice the decorative presentation to every plate of food. What a work of art!

After lunch, Moxie herded everyone to the second large upstairs classroom. All the supplies to make needle-felted pictures were laid out. Moxie had chosen needle felting among many other forms of fiber arts because of its simplicity. No long-winded instructions were needed nor the use of sewing machines. She showed several samples made for the women to see – an abstract, a simple mountain landscape, a bright cheery composition with teacups and hearts, and lastly wildflowers. "Great precision is not necessary with these needle-felted pictures. And remember the house rules, please. What are they?"

Someone from the crowd yelled out, "If you don't know what you are doing – fudge it!" Laughter traveled around the room.

As they worked Moxie had to remind a few women that deep jabs of the needle were not necessary. They were the same women who remarked that it felt like all their frustrations were being worked out in the creation.

At the end of the two-and-a-half-hour session, with a brief afternoon tea and cookie break, Moxie was pleasantly surprised at the outcome. All had done well. Once again, Celeste's was the most remarkable and while Moxie hated to pinpoint one as being better than the other when the opportunity presented itself to talk with Celeste alone, Moxie said to her, "Celeste, for a first-time attempt at needle felting, your piece is quite good."

"You know, Moxie, I always wanted to be an artist. That was always a sticking point between me and my parents. They never encouraged it and it became obvious to me now that I am a sage adult that they wanted me to be created from the same mold as everybody else. It was completely averse to my nature." It was obvious from her pottery piece. She made a coiled bowl well, but then took items that were among the tools, rolled out clay and created embellishments of different shapes to stick on the exterior of the bowl. She was the only in the crowd who didn't do a plain, unembellished coiled bowl, like the sample.

"You don't know how many times I have heard that from other people!" said Moxie.

"Well, I do hope your generation, as they become parents, will be wiser and let their children's gifts from God shine. Yes, sometimes there may be sacrifice but there often is in life. And each of us being different makes for a fascinating world."

"Amen to that!" said Moxie. *You can count on me to remember you and your words*, Moxie thought.

"Ok, everyone. I hope you enjoyed this fiber art craft. Now we are going to switch gears and work with a hard surface. Follow me! We will take an opportunity to stretch and get some fresh air on this beautiful day by going down to the river behind this building and to collect rocks. Let's be quick. Our final activity of the day will be rock painting. Each of you get two rocks, no boulders, mind you!" Moxie then proceeded to encourage the women to paint one rock for themselves to take home and a second with their initials somewhere on it to leave in the garden at Get Your Creative On! "That way your rock will become your testimony of having been here to contribute to an art and wellness community. And while we are outdoors, take time to look at our beautiful gardens. The Way to the Heart Is through the Garden works hard to maintain them for us."

It was a fine way to end what Moxie and Matt felt was a successful first day. Matt and Moxie enjoyed coming together when all participants had gone home.

"Biggest surprise of the day?" Moxie asked Matt.

"Rebecca! My assistant in the kitchen. She was the one who put all those decorative garnishes on the lunch plates. And then when we boxed up the chocolates, she excused herself to go to her car. I thought she wanted to go out for a smoke break or something. When she returned, she said earlier that morning she'd been to the dollar store and had all kinds of stuff in her bag to embellish the chocolate boxes. By the time she finished with them, they looked ready for retail sale not like my feeble attempt with the boxes I sent the NNN people home with. What works of art they were! Far more extensive than I could have done. I am learning from her! She's a keeper and she wouldn't take a cent for the supplies from me. She said it was her pleasure being able to show off her gift-wrapping skills."

"I think she's found her calling right here with us!" said Moxie, suddenly thinking of another workshop possibility.

"How about you, Moxie? What was your biggest surprise of the day?"

"Celeste. You didn't hear her brief but heartfelt story of how she wanted to become an artist, but it was a big sticking point in her relationship with her parents."

"Wow, I think that's all too familiar!" Matt reflected on his own upbringing and his Dad's insistence that any respectable man should have a desk job. Partially why he ended up in real estate after the donut shop.

Chapter 22

"MOXIE, DON'T DO that to yourself."

"Do what, Matt?"

"Beat yourself up for a misjudgment made. Remember, we weren't going to do that – no stressing!"

"Yeah, you're right. Live and learn. And I've learned the pottery workshop was not the best thing to hold here. Too many steps and time involved to get it to a glazed and fired finished product. It would have been the bee's knees to have the raku firing outside here at #48 Union. But transporting the all the equipment needed from barrels to sawdust from the woodworker who made our Get Your Creative On sign made little sense. Glad our eight participants who took the class were ok with going to the Pottery Shed to see the firing or to at least pick up their finished bowls."

"And we need to remember these classes are meant to be introductory only! Wet the tastebuds and explore different types of art, in hopes of finding one's passion," Matt said. "Seeing the Pottery Shed when they go for the raku firing or to pick up their finished works will be another educational experience. So, no harm done."

"This has taught me as new Program Director, I need to go through the paces myself to see what each workshop will entail and not just read a proposal, like I did with the hand building clay workshop. It was so interestingly described that I didn't think to ask enough questions."

"If you go through the steps yourself first before committing to having a workshop here, that's a great opportunity for learning for you too, Moxie."

"Want to experience some of them with me?"

"I'm up for it!" said Matt, looking as if he was glad Moxie asked.

"By the way, I'm working on some other cooking class options and The Worldly Kitchen hopes to collaborate with us in teaching some of them."

"We will be ready in six months."

"If you ever need a taste-tester, you know where to find her."

"Absolutely!"

"Hey, Matt, guess who I got a call from?"

"Who?"

"Celeste. She carried on greatly about her experience here, and she wants to sign up for every workshop we have planned for the next six months."

"Interesting woman. You enjoyed her participation in your fiber arts class, didn't you?"

"Oh, yes! She kept things lively. By the end of day, I think all the women appreciated her quirkiness."

"I hope by the time I'm her age what others think will be less important to me. They say with age, it often happens." Matt chuckled.

Matt had been asking around to see if anyone in the community knew Celeste. From what he found out she was a client of the CFA across the hall who hinted the sky held no limit. Her registering for every class was no problem for her financially. But she struggled to make connections with others. She was, indeed, a one-of-kind individual. After all, Matt quipped, being a star usually did set people apart.

With each session of workshops, routine operations fell into place. The clay hand building workshops were replaced with basic drawing classes. The young woman who taught sketching was as delightful as all the other instructors. When Johanna and Moxie interviewed the woman for the position, she had an unexpected response to one of the questions when they asked her why she was interested in teaching at Get Your Creative On.

"Word has really gotten around town that what you've got going there is a positive experience. As beneficial to the teachers as the students." From the critique forms handed in at the end of each session, the attendees were enjoying the instructors as much as Matt and Moxie enjoyed working with them.

Two separate line-ups of art programs were rotated from week to week but, other than swapping out pottery for drawing, Johanna recommended no other changes until the six-month review. "Otherwise," she said, "assessment of how things are going would be too difficult. If things were constantly being changed, no telling where problems exist. When the six-month review comes around, all four of us who began this venture together will critique all operational issues as well as discuss our future programming. Our financial partners will expect a copy of the review and recommended changes."

One morning, however, the unexpected happened when a new group of participants gathered on the front porch. From her frequent appearances, Matt and Moxie knew Celeste's car when they saw it, and they saw her pull in the parking lot. In fact, she was known to stop by just to say hello whether they were open or not. Their visits were always enjoyable and full of good laughs.

Although her car could be seen in the parking lot, Celeste did not come to join the group on the front porch. Matt, came over to Moxie and whispered, “Where’s your star student?”

Moxie stepped out of the circle of women, and continued the conversation with Matt. “I don’t know. I saw her drive in, but I don’t know what’s taking her so long to get from her car to here.” They waited another five or six minutes. No Celeste.

“Moxie, I’m going out to the parking lot and look in her car. Maybe she needs help.”

Matt did as he said, returned and pulled Moxie aside again. “She’s not in her car. I wonder where she went.”

“Why don’t you go in and get started making truffles with the group. I don’t think we should wait any longer. After all, Celeste has attended several truffle making classes. I’m going around to the back of the property and look for her.”

Matt proceeded indoors with the group and Moxie walked around to the back lawns. She pulled up her hood over her hair to keep it dry from the slight drizzle. She didn’t see Celeste anywhere and had begun to think maybe she’d parked her car in their lot and then had walked up to Main Street. *One last place to look,* thought Moxie, *down by the river.* As soon as Moxie slipped through the small opening in the hedgerow to the lawn that led to the river, she saw Celeste sitting on the bench, her back to Moxie staring at the water tripping over the rocks. Moxie didn't want to frighten her, so she called her name softly. "Celeste." No answer. "Celeste," Moxie said a little louder, "are you not going to join us?"

Celeste turned briefly and then continued to stare at the river. Moxie moved forward and sat on the bench next to her. Celeste had obviously been crying for a while, from the looks of her crumpled up, wet tissue.

"Celeste, what's wrong?" Every time Celeste began to explain she was overcome with sobbing.

Oh dear! thought Moxie. Finally, with some gentle probing, Moxie got out of her what all the tears were about. Her dog of fifteen years, Aurora, had passed away in the night. "Rory was my whole world," sobbed Celeste.

When Celeste's tears finally stopped, Moxie looked at her watch. Thankfully, Moxie's needle felting class was not scheduled until afternoon. "Are you ready to join the others?"

"No, not yet."

"Excuse me just for a minute. I need to call

Matt and tell him I found you." Moxie walked back through the hedgerow and to one side of the yard leading up to the main house and made her call. Then Moxie made a quick call to Pastor Bridges. His voice mail said he was not available and to call his assistant, Rev. Athalia at the given number. Athie answered immediately. "Funny you should call. I am out in your parking lot. I was just stopping in to see how things were going. Neither Rev. Bridges nor I have looked in lately." Moxie explained the situation with Celeste.

"I've got your back," Athie said, "I'll come right around to the bench by the river and speak with Celeste.

Thank you, Jesus, Moxie thought, as she returned to the bench to sit with Celeste until Athie showed up. Athie played unaware and said she'd just stopped by to rob the riverbank of a small rock or two to take home to paint. Moxie got up from the bench, left the two to talk and went inside to see how the truffle making was going.

When Celeste was ready, Rev. Athalia brought her inside to join the group who by then were engaged in the drawing workshop. The Reverend joined in too, to stick around just in case she was needed. However, as Celeste worked on her sketch of her pet companion, Aurora, a beautiful cocker spaniel, you could see a lifting of her spirits through her face and in the positive conversation she was having with the woman sitting next to her.

After the drawing session was over, Athie quietly took her leave. The rest of the day went normally, but the day's event became a necessary discussion point between Johanna, Matt, Moxie and Rev. Bridges that couldn't wait six months to happen. A plan of action was needed for participants, such as Celeste for when they come to the center looking for a way to mend new, raw grief.

At the end of that day, when Moxie said goodbye, Celeste mentioned how helpful it was to put her attention on something creative after her loss the night before. "I feel a bit better already."

"That's what we are here for!" said Moxie and Matt. "See you on Thursday?"

"Yes, definitely!"

Chapter 23

On Thursday, Moxie had catch-up work to do, so after a brief meet and greet, she went directly into her office and stayed there most of the day since she was not scheduled to give any workshops. She joined the group at lunchtime and sat with Celeste and a few others so she could socialize a bit. At the end of the day after Matt had said goodbye to the participants, Moxie heard footsteps on the winding staircase leading up to her office. She figured it was Matt.

"Knock, knock, anyone home?" asked Celeste, as she rapped on the half-closed door. "Oh, come on in Celeste, take a seat." Moxie knew her voice immediately.

Always attractively dressed with touches of artistic flair, Moxie asked, "Hey, where's that beautiful necklace you usually wear? I hope you didn't lose it."

"No, no, I didn't. Not in the right frame of mind to wear it today, that's all. I feel like I've kinda lost my sparkle."

"You? Never!" Celeste gave a brave smile to Moxie's comment. "Yeah, losing a pet can be as devasting as losing a family member. No doubt about it. I'm so sorry Celeste."

"Well, my little Rory, she was the only family I had. She was my sun, my moon and my universe."

"I understand a little of what you are going through. Have you noticed the two portraits down in the front entryway honoring the two women who have in large part made this organization possible?"

"Yes, I certainly have. How can anyone not see them when they walk in. They are gorgeous."

"Well, thank you, I made them. They are Mildred and Eunice. I am proud of the portraits. I appreciate your compliments. Those two women were my sun, my moon and my Universe for many years. They picked me up from the depths of despair and changed my entire life. I'll be forever indebted. Losing them has been tough. But, with time the grief begins to soften."

"Oh, I hope so." Celeste looked out the window squinting at the sun. She brushed her eye with the back of her hand. Moxie was not sure if the bright rays made her tear up or her emotions.

Suddenly it was if Celeste was touched by a spark plug.

"Oh, My God!" she said, "Why look at you! You are one little cutie. Good grief, Pup-Pup! Who in the world made you? You need to come home with me and we can make some wonderful memories together." Moxie didn't know who Celeste was talking to until she rose from her seat and walked over to the table in the corner. She grabbed up one of the stuffed animals Moxie had put there and hugged it as if Aurora aka Rory had returned from the dead. She danced around the room on her tippy toes, twirling circles.

Moxie was so taken by surprise all she could do was watch. When Celeste finally sat back down, she rocked back and forth tightly embracing the stuffed animal, cooing like a baby.

The stuffed animals were proto-types Moxie had made years ago when she was just beginning to sew. She didn't know what to do with the little stuffed dogs and cats, so she'd brought them into her office and displayed them on the table never thinking much about it.

"Celeste, would you like to take that home with you?"

"Oh, can I? I promise I'll give it a good home. See the way these floppy ears are? That's exactly how my little Rory's ears went. They never ceased to charm me. Oh, good grief, Pup-Pup. I need you in my life!" she kissed the little black button nose.

Moxie was so caught off-guard by Celeste's reaction to the stuffed animal it brought the same level of joy to her as a side effect. A smile spread across Moxie's face from ear to ear.

"Oh, I am so wrapped up in this pup-pup, I nearly forgot what I came in here for. Moxie, thank you so much for yesterday. I know sadness from losing my little Rory will come and go unexpectedly but in my talk with Reverend Athie yesterday, I was able to work through a little bit of it. And I know this place will help me too. I've been enjoying these workshops so very much. Thank you."

"I love seeing what you and the rest of the participants are creating here. You know the big, big bay window in the front parlor to the left of the winding staircase? Matt and I have plans to display a revolving showcase of artwork in it so others can see what this creative art and wellness center is all about. If you don't mind me showcasing some of your artistry, I'd love for you to be one of the first featured artists along with your classmates from our opening session. We will switch up the window display every two weeks. What do you think?"

"I'm in!" Celeste said cheerfully.

"In fact, we are going to put strings of little white lights the window so the artwork can be seen in the evening. It will be pretty, and we will announce the featured artists on display on our site and in our social media as well. And once we have accumulated enough participants who have come to workshops here, we hope to use one of our rooms for gallery exhibitions for the public, changing with the seasons."

Celeste left that day with a happier heart, it was evident, as she skipped lightly down the staircase and walked out the door talking to her newfound friend all the way to her car.

Chapter 24

"Where have these past months gone? Five months vanished. Just like that." Matt looked at Moxie and then at Reverend Thad.

"Well, it's not like we've been sitting around twiddling our thumbs!" said Moxie. "Takes a lot of energy to get a project going. It's been exciting though."

"It is hard to believe," said Reverend Thad. "I know I haven't stopped in nearly as frequently as I had hoped, but like you, time has gotten away from me. I've been so grateful Athalia has been able to stop in. She's been the more fortunate one since she's experienced some of the workshops first-hand."

"We were so fortunate Rev. Athie happened to stop in the morning one of our participants had a terrible melt-down over the loss of her dog the night before. She was so helpful, and it was a perfect case of divine timing. And it forced us to put procedural steps in place for future unexpected circumstances such as that. As we've talked before, many of our participants come here looking for a creative experience to heal from something emotional, physical or to seek balance."

"Yes, a precautionary plan is always wise and speaking of unfortunate situations," said Reverend Thad, "I have a church conference I can't miss the week we've scheduled the six-month review of this project. Any objections if I send Athalia in my place since she is familiar with the work that's being done here?

"Of course not!" Moxie answered loudly, she had enjoyed getting to know the Reverends. They blended into the community as well as anyone else in the NNN – all people who were interested in growing a healthy community of citizens not set apart by their Bible thumping, as Miss Eunice used to call it.

"We'd like to hold the meeting on Zoom and of course, invite our sponsors and big supporters to be part of the meeting until we go into the closed executive session at the end. Are you ok with that, Thad?" asked Johanna.

"Sounds great. If we are meeting on Zoom, maybe I can join in after all. But, I will include

Rev. Athalia anyway, just in case I can't join you. Again, she is my back-up if you ever need any kind of pastoral aide in unexpected situations."

"I'll send out an invitation of the meeting details. At Johanna's recommendation, we are planning a special presentation to start our meeting. When looking for financial support for our elevator the Zoom presentation given by Moxie it was a roaring success. Hopefully, what we have planned will be beneficial to the center this time too."

"Are you and Johanna putting together a plan for the next six to twelve months?"

"Yes. We will discuss it in the executive board meeting."

"Sounds great. Look, I've got to run. You two will be coming to the NNN monthly meeting tomorrow evening, at the church, will you not?"

Moxie looked at Matt and nodded her answer. "Sure, we will both be there. Look forward to it."

"Do you need anything? Contributions for a potluck? Or is the usual family cooking for the whole lot of us?"

"Yes, we can depend on them to feed us, and then some. But if you have anything you need test tasters for, bring it along, Matt."

Matt was glad to hear it. He had been

experimenting with a few new dishes, a hearty winter soup and a lunch entrée. Getting some opinions would be helpful.

After the Reverend left, Matt turned to Moxie. "Oh, so I guess from what you said about a surprise opening to our review meeting, you have the go ahead from a few of our past participants to present their testimonials?"

"Celeste is the only one bold enough to agree to give a spoken testimonial. But I have numerous other written testimonials we will put up on the screen as a follow-up to Celeste. And Celeste is aware of that."

"Good plan, Moxie. Knowing Celeste, let's pray she doesn't go off on some wild tangent. This could be a little risky! And she could get a little frisky!"

"Hopefully, we've got that taken care of. Johanna is working with Celeste to coach her a little bit with what to say. So, it will not be completely ad lib. Johanna will give her a time allotment and that should take care of our concerns of her being too long winded. And Johanna and I talked about the importance of not over-coaching Ms. Sparkle. That's part of her charm and we must not take that away. Her beautiful honest candor keeps people engaged. We've seen it here, haven't we?"

"Indeed, we have. I'm rather excited to see what she brings to the stage, frankly."

Matt rose from his chair. Came over to Moxie and did a slap-me-five. "Cheers, housemate! Two more weeks and we've made it through the first six months."

Chapter 25

MOXIE WOKE UP at 3 a.m. with a pounding sinus headache, ringing ears, and her throat felt as raw as the sushi Matt had made for their dinner earlier that night. She got up to get a glass water and thought to herself, *Ain't no way girlfriend! You are not going to work in the morning.* Whatever plague she had she didn't want to spread it.

She walked across the hall and knocked on Matt's bedroom door. There was no answer. *Odd*, she thought, *unless he had some hot date he hadn't told her about and was still out on the town. That being the case, perhaps he skipped town and had gone elsewhere to party.* As far as Moxie knew, Matt was not a barfly. But, how would she know? She and Matt had been so busy getting the Art Center up and running there had been little time for anything else. Moxie went back into her room and sat on the bed pondering. Could it be what Moxie had been suspecting? Or was it, as Eunice used to say, just a fig newton of her imagination without any truth behind it?"

She waited for five or six minutes then got up and went to Matt's door and rapped again. No answer. She put her ear up to the door and listened but didn't hear any noise. She went downstairs and looked out the window. Both cars were there. Matt's was the closest to the house and then Moxie's was parked behind it at the end of the short driveway. *Well*, Moxie thought, *if he's gone anywhere, he's on foot.* But Moxie couldn't imagine him prowling the streets at 3 a.m.

Finally, Moxie got up the gumption to open his bedroom door. "Matt, Matt," she called in, each time a little louder. "Matt," she said one final time, loud enough to rouse him.

He sat straight up and looked at Moxie as if in a fog. "Moxie, is that you? What's wrong?"

"Matt, I feel like crap. I wanted to warn you there is no way I can go to work in the morning. Can you handle things in the Art Center alone?"

"Well, yeah. But how about your workshops? Are you scheduled to give any?"

"No. I had a long to-do list to prepare for the Open House and Garden Party though. Matt, I'm not one to stay in bed and call in sick anymore, but I feel so bad. I am going to listen to myself, I know it's my body telling me to cool it."

"What time is it anyway, Moxie?"

"3:15 a.m."

"Oh...well, can I do anything for you right now?"

"No."

Matt didn't say anything. What he was thinking he knew from living with six sisters he better not call it for what it probably was. So, he posed his question differently, "You must have woken me at three in the morning for some reason. Are you sure I can't do something for you?"

"No, I just wanted you to know you will be on your own tomorrow. I'm going to be indisposed!"

"Indisposed?"

"Yeah, out of commission!"

"Ok well, thanks for the warning. Now both of us can be awake for the rest of the night."

Later that afternoon, Moxie called Matt on the cellphone. "Matt, what did you do? Get out the bull horn and tell everyone in town that I am stricken with some pandemic or something. I haven't gotten any sleep all day. The phone keeps on ringing and everyone wants to know what they can do for me and what can they bring me to eat."

"Only thing I've done is answered one phone call. It was Celeste. She must have set off the spark and now everyone in town knows you are under the weather."

"Moxie, there is a simple solution. Just turn your phone off."

"Oh. I guess I am not thinking too clearly. My head feels as if it's about to burst! My ears are clogged and trying to swallow is painful. Finally, I had to start saying to all the callers, 'The only thing I want is Matt's prize-winning Chicken Soup.' Then they all say, 'Well, we can't help you with that.' I also told everyone they can help me by staying away, as far as possible, so I don't give them the crud. I nip it in the bud by asking, 'You don't want to catch it and miss out on our Open House and Garden Party, do you?' That seems to put the kibosh on them wanting to come over."

"Moxie, I have been cooking up some chicken soup for you here in the kitchen. I was just getting ready to bring it over."

"Have you really? Oh Matt, that's so thoughtful of you."

"Don't mention it. We need to get you better! We've got a big day coming up. I went to your desk and found your to-do list. I and some of the NNN folks have ticked off a few items to lighten the burden."

"Awww...you are all so nice!"

"Moxie, that's what friends are for!"

“I know Matt, but you know me. Before Eunice and Mildred came along, I was so used to fending for myself, help is not an easy thing for me to accept.”

“Well, young lady, you better get used to it! I’ll be over with that soup in a few minutes.”

Chapter 26

"ARE WE ALL SET?" Matt asked, as he looked around the room at Moxie, Johanna, and the two Reverends?

"Yep!" said Johanna, "Let her rip. Go live with the pre-recorded video."

> "Hello, my name is Celeste B. Bright. When I arrived at Get Your Creative On, my name was Adalyte. I hope you'll listen in to my story. I wanted to go to art school rather than to a traditional college, but my parents wouldn't hear of it. Then, I got married right out of college and kept busy with my babies. Perhaps this sounds familiar. Anyway, long story short, finally my time in life had come. I had a life-long creative yearning that I needed to fulfill. So, I set my intentions, excuse me while I do that, I must turn them on, she

said reaching for the clasp at the back of her neck and drawing her beautiful lit-up necklace out from her between her cleavage into view. Any who, at Get Your Creative On they call me their star student. I have found more sparkle in my life from taking the art workshops at Get Your Creative On then I have ever had in my life.

"However, one day at the art center, I arrived feeling miserable. The night before my little dog of fifteen years passed away. I was beyond sad, deep into it, and felt like my life was over. I sat with my sadness down by the river behind the art center and talked with one of the community human resources they partner with here. It was a rough day, and I was having a rough time. I worked through a few issues and felt a little more stable. Enough to join in with the workshops that were going on.

"By the end of the day, I was feeling infinitely better, and I came to understand first-hand how "Art is a wound turned into light." Celeste picks up her stuffed animal Rory and embraces it. "One fiber artist associated with Get Your Creative On brought this notion clear to me through her work of art. I found this handmade folk-art animal sitting in the corner when I went to Get Your Creative On. 'Good grief, Pup-Pup!!! You're coming home with me,' I said when I saw the little cutie. I fell instantly in love with this artful creation, Aurora or 'Rory' I call her, after my dog who died. To conclude, joy and light has arrived back in my life. That is what art is all about."

Then Celeste danced out of the video, twirling circles on her tippy-toes hugging her Good grief, Pup-Pup!!!© just as she did when she found her new love on that sad day in her life.

Before the text of the other testimonials began to roll across the screen, the two Reverends looked at one another. "We've got our spokeswoman and a model student," said Moxie "Yup! An elevator of a different kind!" said Johanna. Matt and the two reverends smiled broadly.

Matt whispered, "Shhh...check this out," and he pointed to words on the screen.

"I arrived at Get Your Creative On rather dubious. After all, I've had years of traditional therapy due to trauma in my life. *How could making art do anything for me?* I thought. *I'm still working on some issues for sure. But I have to admit, I feel much closer to having a wholesome mindset.* Get Your Creative On has made a difference. I've been able to lose myself and find myself all at the same time. I'd like to say I can't explain what has happened through the creative process, but I hope this center is around for a long, long time. If it has been this helpful to me, I am sure it will be to others. What a beneficial resource for the health of the community. Thank you, Get Your Creative On! You rock!!" ~ "Isabelle," 21 years old.

A few more short testimonials appeared on the screen, one at a time. When they were over, Johanna went live and Moxie thanked all the partners, supporting organizations and the Neighbor-to-Neighbor Network, at large, for tuning in to the Zoom presentation. "Now the closed executive session will begin." Matt, being the administrator for his Zoom account was able to close-down connection with those not included in the executive session.

Johanna as leader of the meeting, allowed time for free and open discussion of the video and testimonials they had all witnessed.

"May I say a few words before we begin

discussing our set agenda?" Everyone knew what that meant so the four in the room bowed their heads.

"Father, we are grateful for the creativity that you give to each-and-every one of us. We give thanks for what is a growing important resource in our community. Steer us and those who need to find us so we can be a ray of light in their darkness. Amen."

"Thank you, Thad. Let's begin," said Johanna. "You've all gotten our proposed budget for the next six months ahead of time as well as an overview of expenditures and income. Hopefully, you have had time to review them." All shook their heads affirmatively. Johanna took the agenda and ran with it, item by item.

#1 "I'd like to make a motion to increase our programs, and we've all already seen Moxie's list of potential new programs. I would also like to increase the number of days we are open to four days a week. Any objections?" There were none, so they moved on.

#2 "As you all are aware, next week, the town begins removing all trees from the north-side of the sidewalk along the northside of this property. It will be necessary for us to remove overgrown shrubs and trees on our property as well, because the wires have become entangled. So, we will need to relandscape the grounds over on the north end so this place doesn't lose its curbside appeal. Any thoughts or ideas?" When no one came forward with any earthshaking suggestions, they all decided it would be best to sleep on it and table it for the next month's meeting.

#3 "Now we need feedback from the Community Church whether our mission is being fulfilled." Thad spoke about how the center was a complimentary component to the work the church does. The art center had served a good number of participants who came at the suggestion of one of the pastors. Such as Rebecca – Matt's terrific kitchen assistant. She'd become so valuable the Executive Committee agreed with Matt's desire to give her more hours, responsibility and creative license outside of the kitchen.

#4 The development of specialty food products was approved by the Board at the six-month review with several requirements. Matt was asked to start very slowly to test the waters using the label *From the Kitchen of: Get Your Creative On*. The committee was pleased to hear Matt had already gotten commitments from local garden markets to provide produce for the canned and jarred products. And for the future canning workshops.

#5 The proposed window gallery displaying

participants work had no objections. Matt mentioned how he and Moxie had planned to put Rebecca in charge of that. They knew she had it in her to run with it and do a fabulous job.

When the executive session ended, all voiced their confidence that what they had planned for the next six months would be even better. It was agreed they were off to a wonderful start and looked forward to the First Annual Open House and Garden Party one week away.

Chapter 27

"HOW YOU FEELING, HON?" asked Patience, the drawing instructor and soon to be muralist.

"Thanks for asking, Patience I feel much better. Not quite 100% but almost there." Only Moxie knew what Matt's prize-winning chicken soup and the bouquet of flowers he brought to her did for her spirit. The combination of coneflowers, yarrow and foxglove were gorgeous, and she asked Patience to paint some of them into her wall mural composition. Moxie was so happy to give the art commission to Patience. She was a warm person, detail-oriented and very dedicated to her young art career. She needed just the right opportunity as a stepping-stone toward bigger things professionally. Moxie had high hope the commission was going to launch Patience into a full-time career as a muralist. The drawback was the possibility of losing her as an instructor. But there were other talented people in the area who could teach basic drawing. The way Moxie saw it, Get Your Creative On was valuable for propelling young instructors forward into full-time art careers or as a great place for those who have had busy art careers and want to slow things down as they got older. Part time employment was perfect for either.

"Oh, Patience, I meant to tell you the tree people were here while I was under the weather, and I still have not gotten around to the other side of the building to see what it looks like. Do you want to walk around and see it with me?"

"Sure!" said Patience. She didn't have the heart to tell Moxie she'd already seen it because she had a feeling Moxie was going to be taken by surprise. Patience figured if she didn't overreact then perhaps Moxie wouldn't either.

Matt tried to be diplomatic when he said, "Moxie's eyebrows get raised easily," but what Patience took it to mean was Moxie was a bit of alarmist. Matt said, "Don't even mention what things look like over there and let Moxie see it for herself and form her own opinions."

Maybe, Patience thought, *I've put Matt's comments about Moxie in the wrong context.*

Moxie and Patience chatted while they walked, and when they arrived on the northside of the building, Patience heard Moxie gasp. *Uh-oh,* thought Patience, *here it comes.*

"Oh, Good Lord! They've raped this whole side of our property. So much for any privacy and all charm has gone out the window. This is awful. I could just cry! And why did the town schedule to take down all the trees right before our garden party?"

Patience tried to console the inconsolable with platitudes. "Oh, you'll get used to it." Moxie looked at Patience with graven eyes full of doubt. "It's just a shock because it's so different than what you are used to." Finally, Patience hit the right words, "Teamwork makes the dream work, Moxie. You've seen my renderings, between what I have planned and what the garden and landscape center has planned you are going to have a very organic piece of art that is going to be the envy of town. And with all those trees removed along the road, the artwork will get noticed by every passing car. You know what that means, don't you?"

"What?"

"It means people who normally don't visit art galleries and places like this may just get a taste for art."

"You mean become artsy-fartsy?"

"Well yes, I suppose you could call it that.

But I'm trying to say they could potentially become your customers or even better, your supporters."

"Good point! Well, I do hope the garden center has some plants or shrubs or something that is fast growing so the vacancy of all privacy we used to have won't be so in the face."

"They do! I've already spoken with Heather about it. Moxie, let go! You'll be pleased with the end result. I promise you."

"Hey," Moxie said, "Did you see what else the tree company did while they were here? It's fantastic and it was a surprise to me because I was laid up sick and Matt gave them permission. And they said no extra charge. We have an awful lot of kind and creative people in this world, Patience. People like you. Come on around to the front of the house."

Moxie pointed to the big bay window. "They trimmed the Devils Darning Needles, the encroaching vine, around the window so we can use the big window as art exhibit space that people will see when passing by on the sidewalk. I love how they trimmed the vine to make a lovely organic frame using the Clematis Virginiana. What do you think?"

"Looks great! I can't believe I didn't notice it this morning when I drove in. I look forward to seeing some of my students work hanging in the window!"

"That's the plan. And at night it will be lit by strings of small white lights."

"Cool!" said Patience. "That will be very attractive."

"Won't it?"

Later that evening, Moxie considered Patience's words about letting go and trusting the outcome of the wall mural. *Afterall,* she asked herself, *hadn't she decided to trust when she uprooted herself, moved to a new community, and then took on this project?* Yes, she had! And things had gone along even better, albeit quite differently, than she could have ever expected.

Chapter 28

JOHANNA, MATT, MOXIE and the Reverends Thad and Athalia mingled among the crowd on the back lawn of the Art Center. Seeing Amity and Galen from Merciful Touch, the wellness center Johanna took Moxie to outside of town came as a big and welcomed surprise. The crew from the garden center and garden café were all there too.

Moxie was happy she and her cohorts decided to start the 1st Annual Open House and Garden Party at 5 p.m. and have drinks and heavy d'oeuvres rather than a seated dinner party. "Summer is all about frivolity," one of the NNN members, wisely said, when he argued for a less formal event. People were decked out in everything from authentic garden party wear like Moxie, with floral dresses and wide-brimmed garden hats, to the more casual dressy shorts or capris and flip-flops. That was what Moxie liked about being in a town further from a city. From what she had observed as a newcomer, it seemed like people were less boxed into certain expectations or high-falutin' standards. Some weeks ago, Celeste had echoed what Eunice often said, "It's a freeing feeling to be able to nurture one's nature."

The lawns and grounds looked beautiful. Moxie admired the festive decorations. Rebecca had outdone herself in leading a group of volunteers in pulling it all together. Headline and picture worthy! Rebecca was overflowing with talent and welcomed any opportunity to use it.

Moxie decided to wander to the river where it looked like people were gathering. She entered through the arched opening in the newly clipped and trimmed boxwood hedgerow. Matt was wise to have taken the suggestion of the tree company to tame the wild hedge into a topiary gateway leading to the river. Rather than look like an overgrown mess, it now looked like an entryway to a proper secret garden.

Kirk, the kitchen shop owner had his guitar in hand and was sitting on one of the boulders streamside. He strummed slowly and sang softly "Through the hedge, to the river's edge, hold my arm, safety from harm." Moxie took in the site and decided to stroll back to the tent to make sure the food was being set out. She felt flooded with emotion as if on a high. What a satisfying feeling to get the Art Center to this point, a year into it. It was a day for celebration.

Sometime later after Moxie had checked that all was going as scheduled, Athie came over to Moxie in the tent. “What a stellar June evening we have for this. Perfect weather for the first Open House and Garden Party. Did you see the folks sitting on the rocks down by the river?”

“Yeah, I did, Athie. Wonderful, isn’t it? Everyone really seems to be enjoying themselves so much.”

"Did you see when little Ms. Twinkle Toes was jumping from boulder to boulder with her necklace all aglow?”

“No! Was she really? With shoes on or off?”

“Off! I was even there to witness when she landed in the water up to her neck.”

“Get out! Are you teasing me?”

“No, really! She sure baptized herself and then she came up with a priceless corker. She got out of the water with Kirk’s assistance, laid herself flat out on her back in the grass and said, “Now I lay me down to dry, night fall is nearly thine, so shine...shine...shine.”

“Ha, ha, ha! Oh, that woman sure has added a lot of fun to this place. So where is Celeste now?”

"Oh, she ran out to her car to get a change of clothes she just happened to bring along. She's in the lady's room now. I hope her beautiful necklace wasn't ruined."

Athie and Moxie stood watching all the activity. There was gaiety everywhere. Uproarious laughter came from groups playing croquet and bocci. Other people danced to the melodious live music under the tent where the food was.

"It's so good to see people when they've let their hair down. I hate to break things up, but a few people have some words to say. I'd like to rally them in before people begin to disappear." Athie didn't think anyone was getting ready to go anywhere except to the tables to get more food and drink. But she went over to the band leader and got wireless mic, as well as everyone's attention. Then she handed the mic off to the head of the NNN who had gone to the front of the tent. Soon chairs began screeching on the wooden dance floor and people started taking seats under cover.

"I just wanted to say a warm welcome to all and thank you for coming. Moxie from Get Your Creative On has some words and then Matt will follow her up." Moxie rose and went to the podium.

"Good evening, I will make this brief. I just wanted to say thank you to the NNN and all of our partners and supporters for helping us to Get Your Creative On up on its feet and running. Our two figureheads, Eunice and Mildred would be so proud of what we have accomplished.

"I hesitate to mention any names, because there is not a business in this network who has not contributed, some with financial contributions and others with much needed services-in-kind. For instance, Stitching Joy, the knitting shop, provided needles and yarn for the beginners knitting classes, Words that Heal, the book store, provided journals for our writing workshop and pens came from the stationery shop, Parchment Papers, for the introductory calligraphy classes. The Worldly Kitchen donated kitchen supplies so we can create the food we feed our workshop participants. The women's clothing shops, All Dun Up and Artful Threads have given workshops on color and how it affects our moods. So many of our NNN members have provided goodies for the gift bags we send home with our workshop participants ...I could go on and on.

"But I'd especially like to say thanks to our heavy lifters — The Way to the Heart Is Through the Garden, their commitment of time and employees to keep our lawns and gardens beautiful has been beyond what we could have ever expected. Every one of you know what your contributions have been without me listing them. Big or small, we are grateful for them all because you are all partners in community with us."

Moxie left the front and went to sit with Matt and Johanna. Matt leaned over close enough until their shoulders were touching. "Hey lady," he whispered, "your moxie is getting bolder. It's quite attractive and so is your new outfit." Her face reddened and she was so grateful she didn't have to give any more speeches that evening because she felt like she'd come unraveled.

"Matt, come on up," said the chair of the NNN. Matt went to the front and took the mic.

"Many of you may have traveled down Middle Street to get here and you may have seen the draping on the far side of the building. Tonight, we are having an unveiling of public art right here on our property. If you will all follow me, we will have a short ceremony. Take your time as you walk over. We don't want anyone else falling. Everyone's eyes landed on Ms. Sparkle who had a different set of clothes and bright smile on. This does not, and I repeat NOT, indicate an end to this party. We have plenty more food and drink and we want you to stick around until we push you out. Also, if anyone is interested, we will have the artist's rendering displayed on a table in this tent after the unveiling. The drawings are quite interesting with several overlays. When one person on the Executive Committee session saw the renderings, he said he was so taken by the design that if the budget didn't allow for it, he'd personally pick up the slack. It was music to the ears of all, especially Moxie who had taken a leap of faith and made it happen even though we'd tabled the project until next year thinking it might be a little too ambitious. Thanks to our artist who donated her labor and to the wonderful folks who supplied the cherry picker lift so Patience had a strong platform to stand on and could be at the level where she needed to work. All of this reduced our costs for this public art. We did not need to have anyone take up the slack and Moxie got it done! Kudos! Maybe we will hit up that generous offer some other time!" Everyone had a good chuckle.

"Meet you all over on the far side of the building along Middle Street," Matt said as he led the way. Once everyone gathered, Matt picked up the mic again. "I'd like to introduce the artist, Patience, who teaches our basic drawing and painting classes. As you will see this wall mural is anything but basic and there is a lot unique about it."

Matt turned to the artist. "Patience can I put you on the spot and ask you to tell us more about your creation?"

"Sure!" said Patience full of enthusiasm, taking the mic from Matt. "Aside from the elements of 'trompe l'oeil' I have incorporated into the mural, this piece of art will look different through each season and each year, just as we all do, as what is around it grows, blooms then withers. Again, I invite you to look at the renderings when we are finished here. As you will see from the overlays, this is very literally organic art at its best. Thank you to The Way to the Heart Is Through the Garden for your special contribution to this fine art piece. I love the natural transition which incorporates a variety of plantings and the stone building right into the mural."

"Now, I will let Heather. the plant specialist, tell you more." Patience handed the mic to Heather.

"By this time next summer, the people in the mural will look like they are sitting in the middle of a botanical park doing different kinds of art. But there will be new garden treasures in the dark seasons of fall and winter to enhance and bring additional color and a different sort of life to the mural. I look forward to seeing it unfold and as the plantings and topiaries mature, the art will become even more interesting and eye-opening."

Then came a huge standing ovation. Matt took the mic once more. "Without further ado, Athie and Thad, climb on up Jacob's ladders and drop the drape!" Matt extended his hand in the direction of the side of the building where the ladders were placed.

Athie turned to the crowd. "I'm afraid of heights but am doing this as an opportunity for self-growth. Please pray for me. Will you?" Matt and Moxie, the spotters, bowed their heads before she began to climb the rungs. And as she rose Matt could hear her whispered plea, "Lord, if I fall, catch me please."

True to the artist's renderings the mural displayed people sitting on curved stone benches in a semi-circle doing various kinds of arts - a man knitting, a teen drawing, a child with her easel with paint, an old woman whittling, a man dancing a jig while playing the violin. Quite ingenious was the work of the artist to fool the eye into making the benches look rounded and the scene multi-dimensional on a one-dimensional stone wall surface.

"Wow! This is fabulous!" echoed many voices. A passing car pulled up to the curb just as the mural was unveiled and tooted its horn. Plants, flowers and shrubs had already begun to naturally embrace and contribute to the wall mural's attractiveness. The chair of the NNN came forward.

"What do you think folks? It's the best piece of promotion we could ever have as people come down #48 Union from the north going southbound or travel west to east on Middle or vice-versa. And here we are right on the corner of Middle and Union."

The party continued until sundown, at which time, all who were left Moxie, Matt, Johanna and the two Reverends all said how they'd enjoyed themselves. The pastors begged goodnight; but Johanna would not let them leave.

"Oh, Matt and Moxie, there is something we've been meaning to talk with you both about," said Johanna.

"Uh-oh, Matt, here comes the axe!" said Moxie. The others laughed.

"Seeing how where you two work is all about wellness, we are concerned that you don't suffer from burn-out. It happens to the best of us you know."

Moxie and Matt both shook their heads; both well acquainted with burn-out. "We are not suggesting this, we are demanding it for your own good health. You've both done a remarkable job of getting the art center going. We are going to require you two to shut the doors for a well-deserved vacation, all expenses paid by a generous travel agency and some others in town. Take a two-week break for R & R."

Moxie was taken by surprise but noticed the

amused look on Matt's face. "Are we supposed to take a break separately or together?" asked Matt.

"Well, I don't know," said Johanna. "Our friend Eunice told me before she went on to a new life, to never get in the way of Saints. 'Let them do the work,' she said. So, perhaps I'd better let St. Andrew figure it out and do what he does best. But, I am your sister, Matt, so maybe it's ok if I have something to say about that."

"We are not going there!" said the two Reverends, their guffaws could be heard behind their hands.

"Wait a minute, you guys," Moxie said. "I feel as if I have been left out of a private joke." She looked at Matt and then Johanna and then back and forth again.

"Oh my God," Moxie said as she realized something. "Why haven't I ever noticed before? You two have many similar features! Are you brother and sister?"

"Irish twins!" The two said at the same time, laughing. "Two siblings born within one year from the same mother." Moxie looked at Johanna's full head of gray hair and Matt's deep chocolate hair, doubting.

"Hold on," said Matt, "we don't look the same age, or do we?" Moxie was not going to put her foot in her mouth, so she said nothing.

"Moxie, meet my oldest sister of six, Johanna."

Well, thought Moxie, *I guess I can put all foolish notions I was forming in my mind about the two of them, to bed, right here and now.*

Amen!

Won't you be a good neighbor
and tell others about this story?

Acknowledgements

So many friends and neighbors whom I have known throughout my lifetime are represented in this publication in many small ways. Artists of all kinds inspire me daily to continue writing and to work at perfecting my craft. I am so grateful for the encouragers and mentors I have found in the art and faith communities who enrich my life.

I'd like to thank Jan and Joe McDaniel of BookCrafters. Once again, thank you for your publishing assistance. You are so easy to work with!

My gratitude to Karen McLane of PostNet for her graphic design skills in bringing her cover art to this book. Your input is greatly appreciated.

And to my entire family, thanks for your patience with me as I continued to write my heart out.

Books by
Award-Winning Author
Sue Batton Leonard

Fiction:

- *Sew the Heart*
  Book #1 Neighbor to Neighbor Series
- *Heart for Community*
  Book #2 Neighbor to Neighbor Series

Biography:

- *Richard Galusha: An Artist's Journey*
  Finalist Eric Hoffer Book Award

Memoir:

- *Gift of a Lifetime: Finding Fulfilling Things in the Unexpected*
- 2 EVVY Book Awards
- Harvest Book Award

eBook:

- *Lessons of Heart & Soul* – Short Stories

Contributing Author:

- *Wounded Healers – Women of the Way Ministries*